DATE DUE

JAN 28			
JAN 28			
FEB 10			
APR 06			
APR 22			
JAN 24			
APR 17			
AUG 31 SEP 08			
SEP 23			
SEP 30			
MAR 19			

Demco, Inc. 38 293

Zinc ALLOY
SUPER ZERO

Librarian Reviewer
Katharine Kan
Graphic novel reviewer and Library Consultant, Panama City, FL
MLS in Library and Information Studies, University of Hawaii at
Manoa, HI

Reading Consultant
Elizabeth Stedem
Educator/Consultant, Colorado Springs, CO
MA in Elementary Education, University of Denver, CO

STONE ARCH BOOKS
www.stonearchbooks.com

Graphic Sparks are published by Stone Arch Books
151 Good Counsel Drive, P.O. Box 669
Mankato, Minnesota 56002
www.stonearchbooks.com

Library of Congress Cataloging-in-Publication Data
Lemke, Donald B.
Super Zero / by Donald Lemke; illustrated by Douglas Holgate.
p. cm. — (Graphic Sparks. Zinc Alloy)
ISBN 978-1-4342-0762-3 (library binding)
ISBN 978-1-4342-0858-3 (pbk.)
1. Graphic novels. [1. Graphic novels. 2. Heroes—Fiction. 3. Robots—Fiction. 4. Bullies—Fiction.] I. Holgate, Douglas ill. II. Title.
PZ7.7.L33Su 2009
[Fic]—dc22 2008006712

Summary: Zack Allen loves comic books, but he's nothing like his favorite superheroes. He's always getting picked on by bullies at school. Then one day, Zack builds a high-tech robot suit. Now he must decide how to use his newfound powers. He has become Zinc Alloy, the world's newest superhero!

Art Director: Heather Kindseth
Graphic Designer: Brann Garvey

1 2 3 4 5 6 13 12 11 10 09 08

Printed in the United States of America

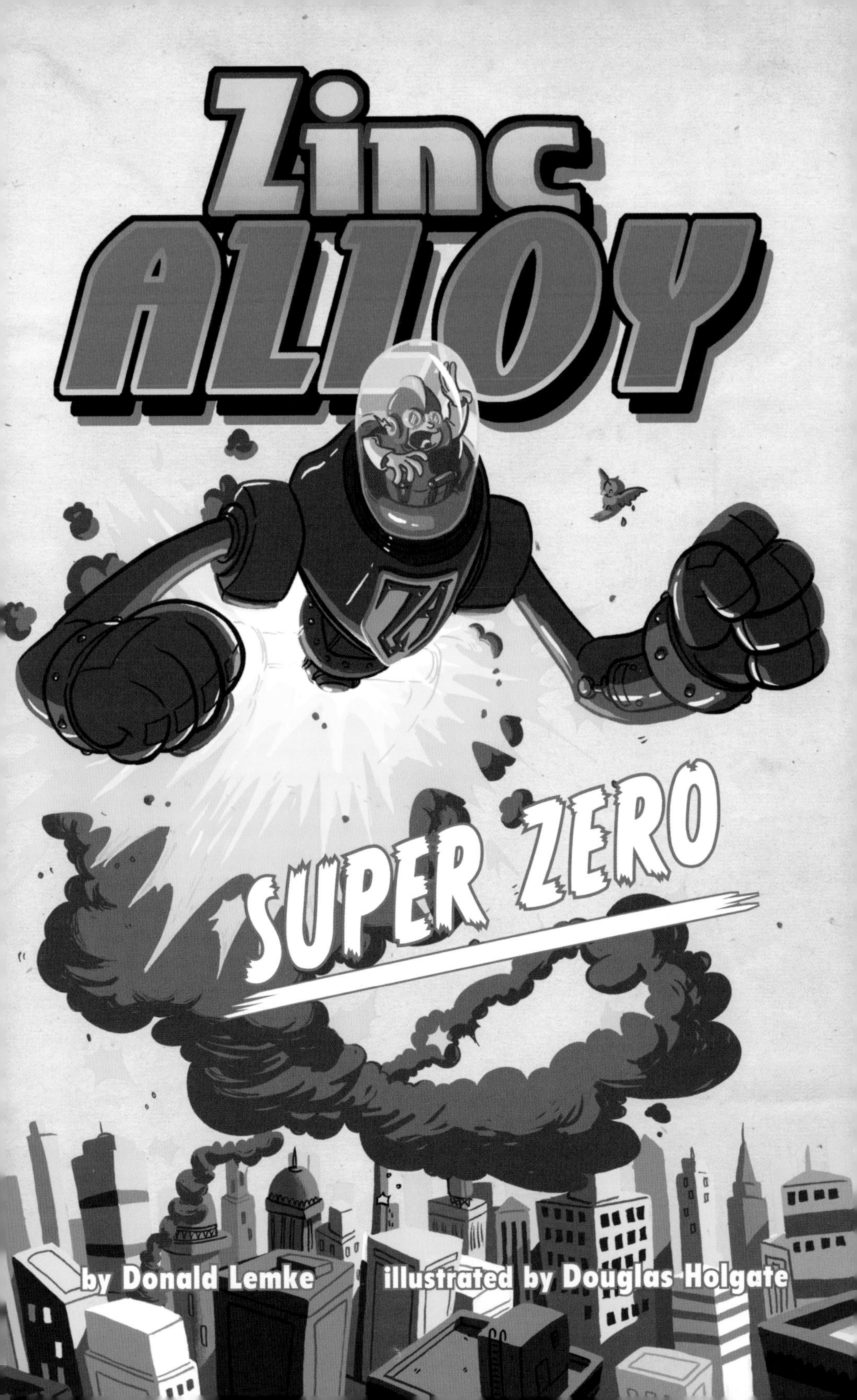
Zinc
ALLOY
SUPER ZERO
by Donald Lemke
illustrated by Douglas Holgate

Cast of CHARACTERS

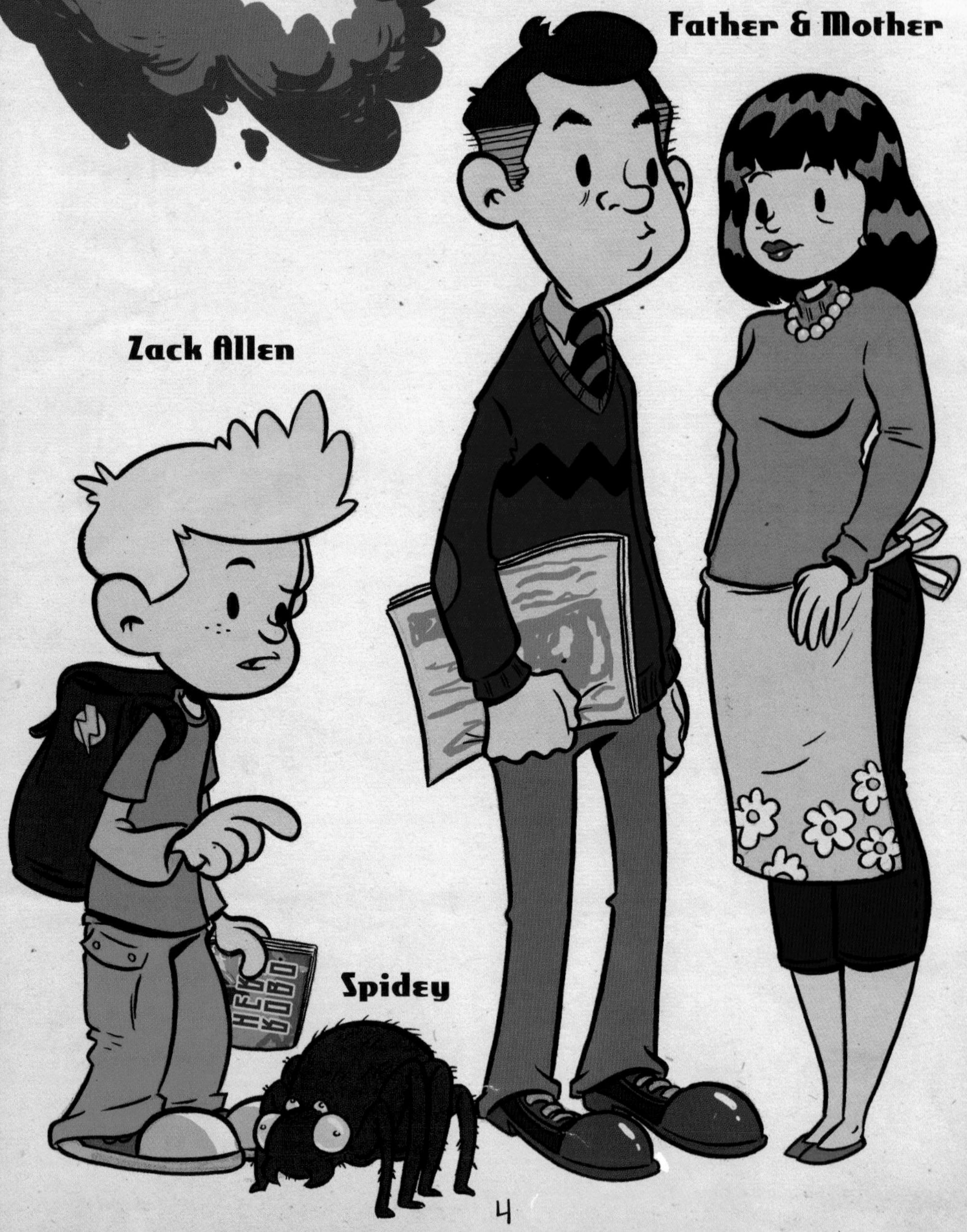
Father & Mother
Zack Allen
Spidey

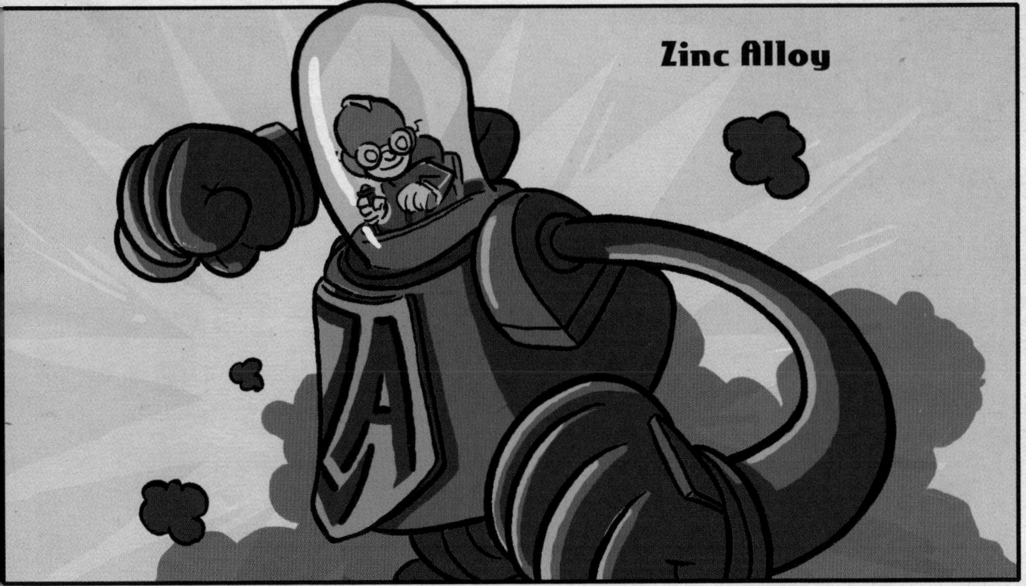
Zinc Alloy

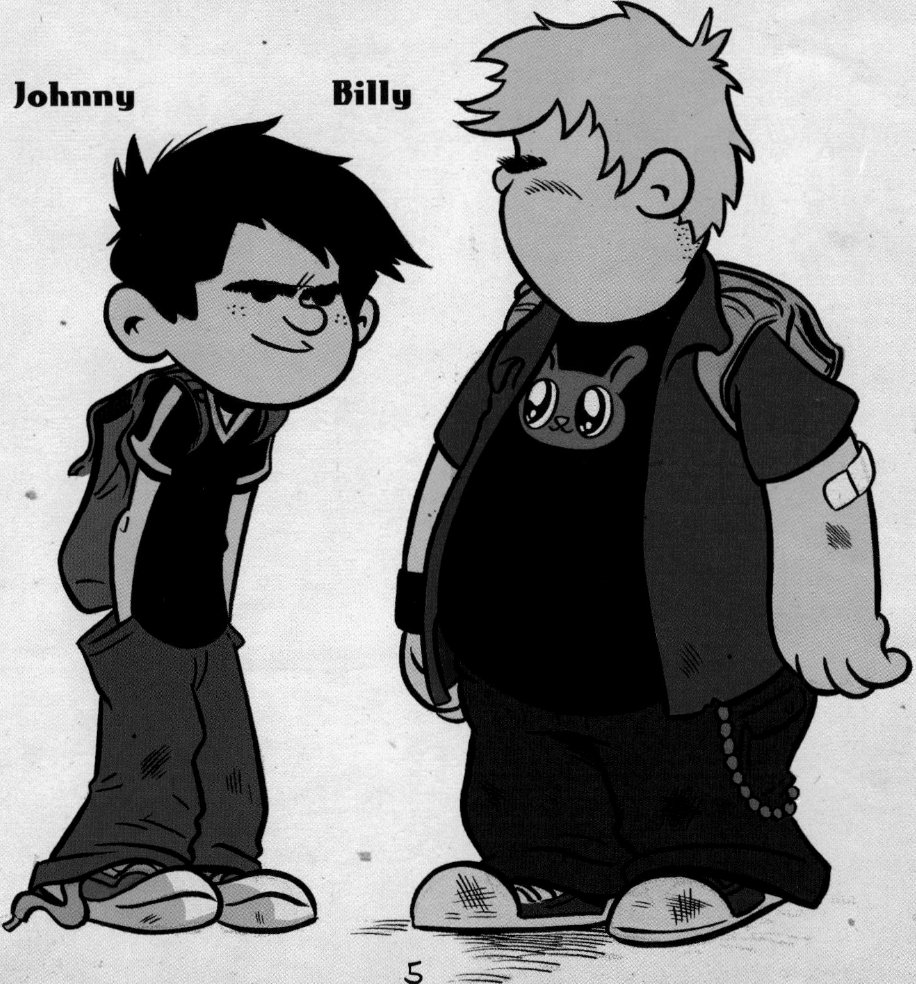
Johnny
Billy

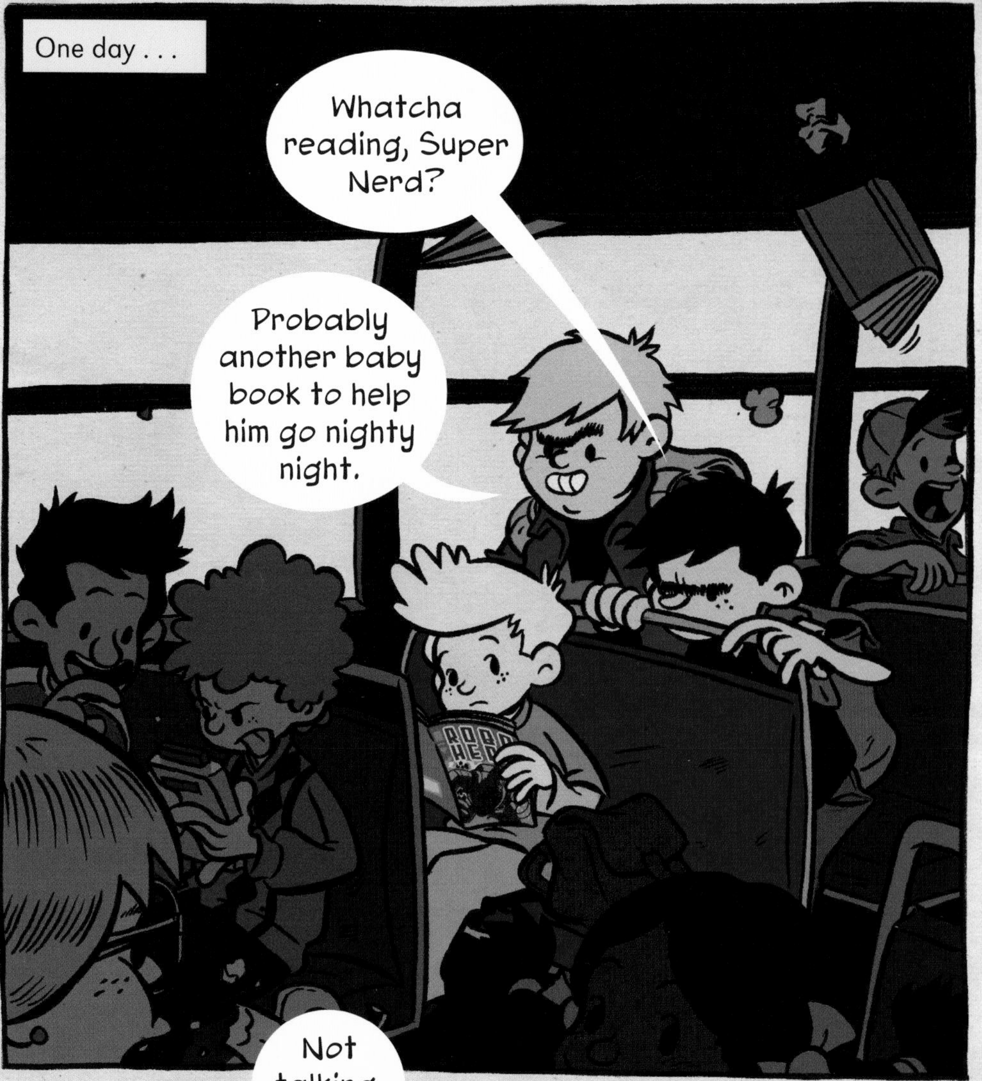
One day . . .
Whatcha reading, Super Nerd?
Probably another baby book to help him go nighty night.

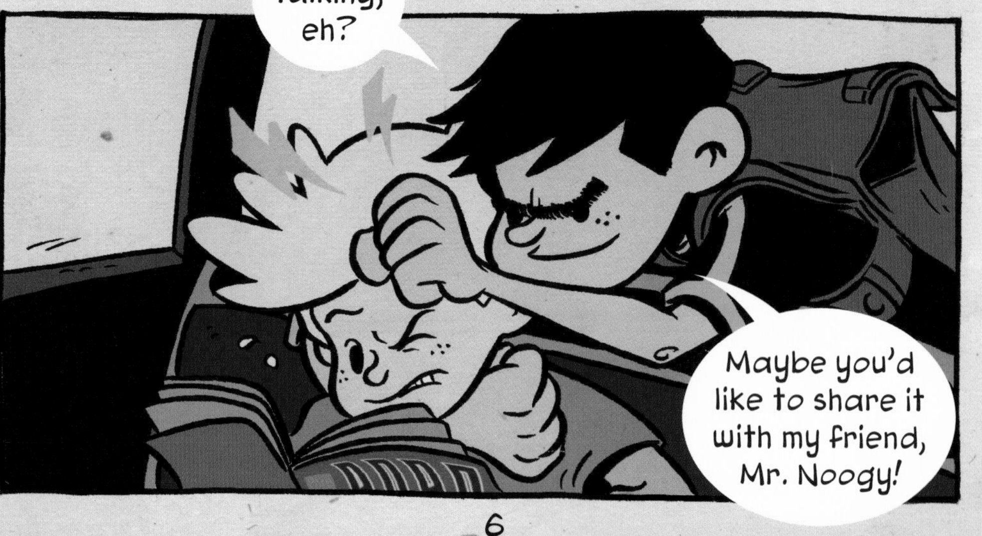
Not talking, eh?
Maybe you'd like to share it with my friend, Mr. Noogy!

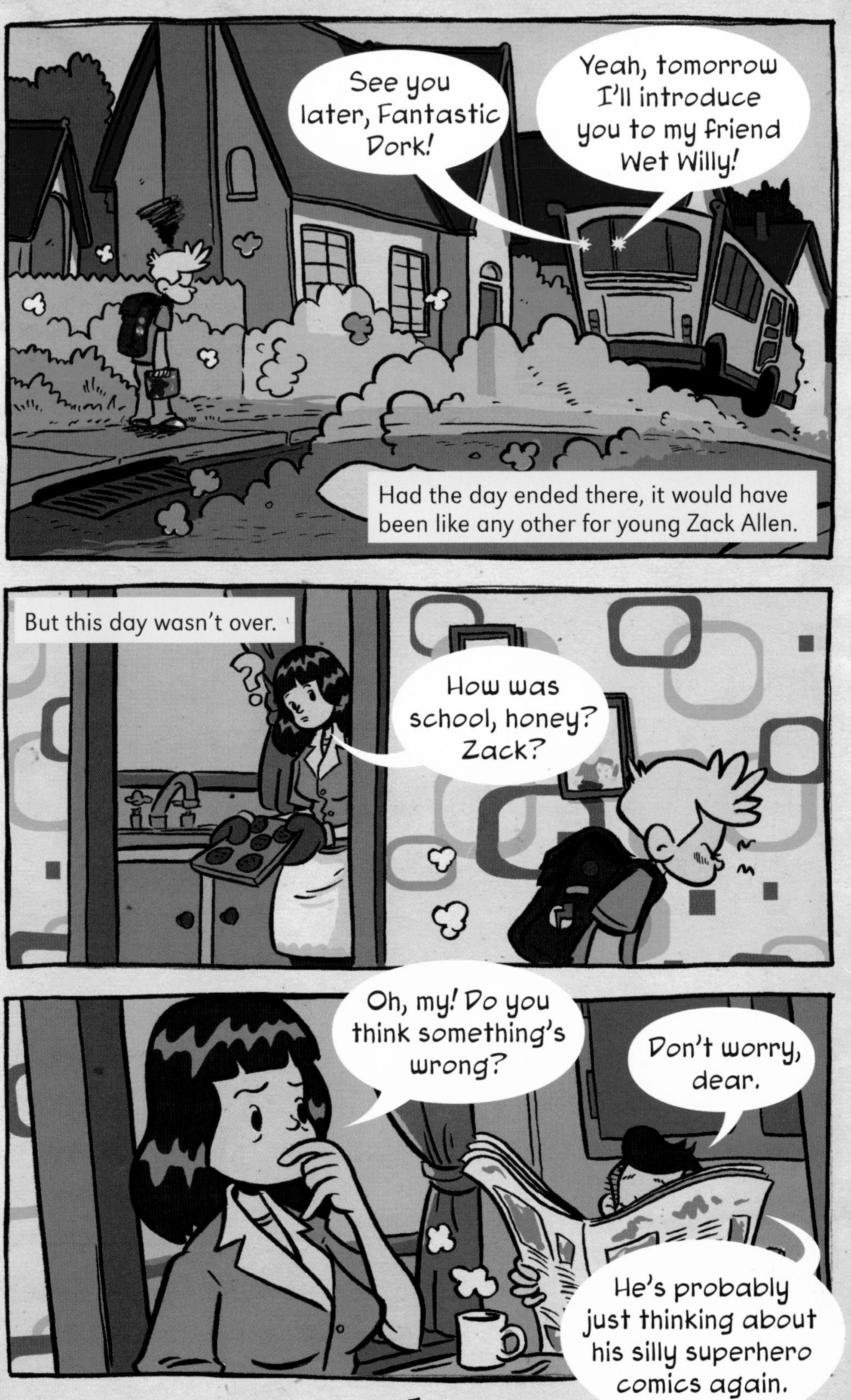

See you later, Fantastic Dork!
Yeah, tomorrow I'll introduce you to my friend Wet Willy!
Had the day ended there, it would have been like any other for young Zack Allen.
But this day wasn't over.
How was school, honey? Zack?
Oh, my! Do you think something's wrong?
Don't worry, dear.
He's probably just thinking about his silly superhero comics again.

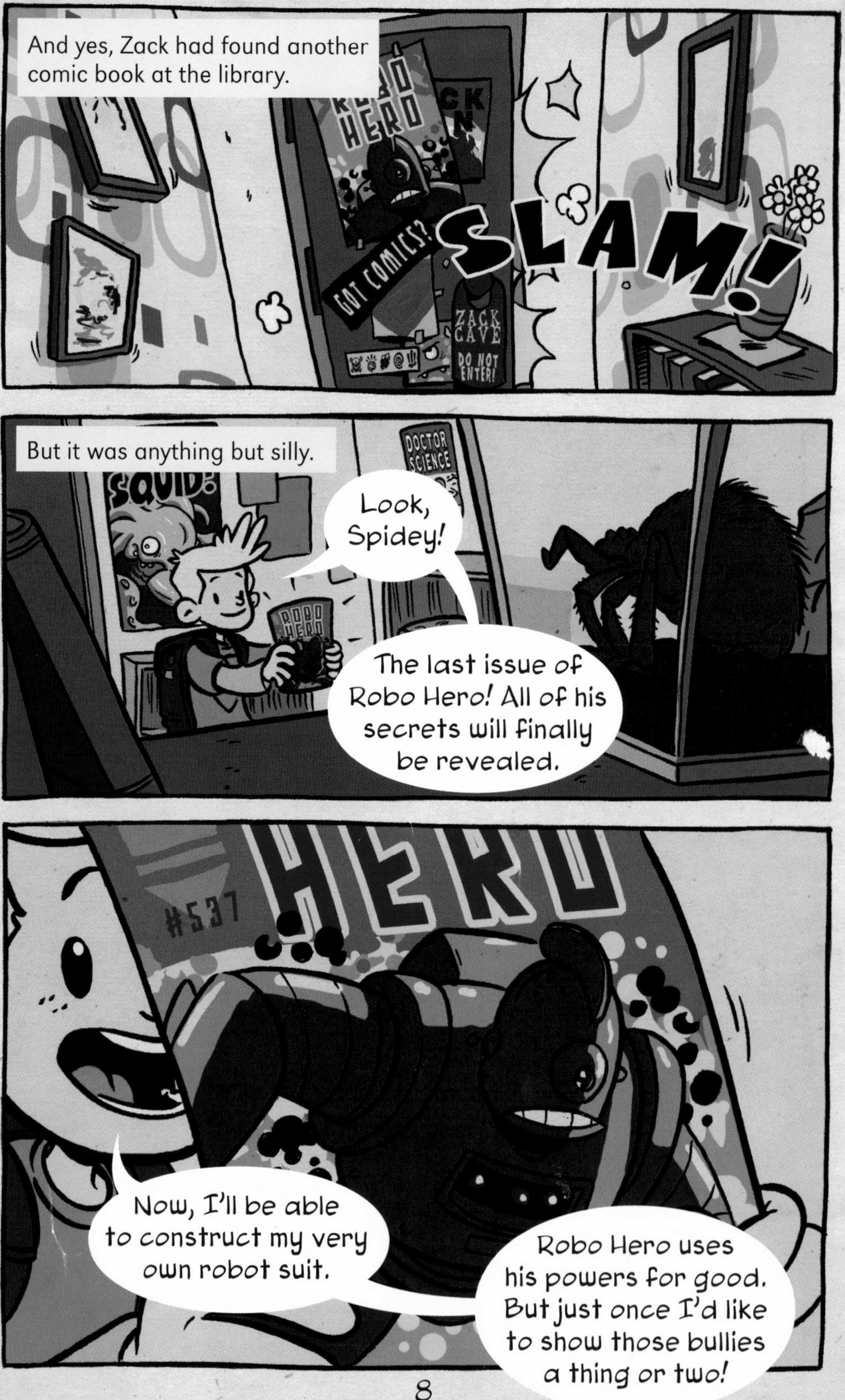
And yes, Zack had found another comic book at the library.
ROBO HERO
GOT COMICS?
ZACK CAVE
DO NOT ENTER!
SLAM!
But it was anything but silly.
SQUID!
DOCTOR SCIENCE
Look, Spidey!
The last issue of Robo Hero! All of his secrets will finally be revealed.
HERO
#537
Now, I'll be able to construct my very own robot suit.
Robo Hero uses his powers for good. But just once I'd like to show those bullies a thing or two!

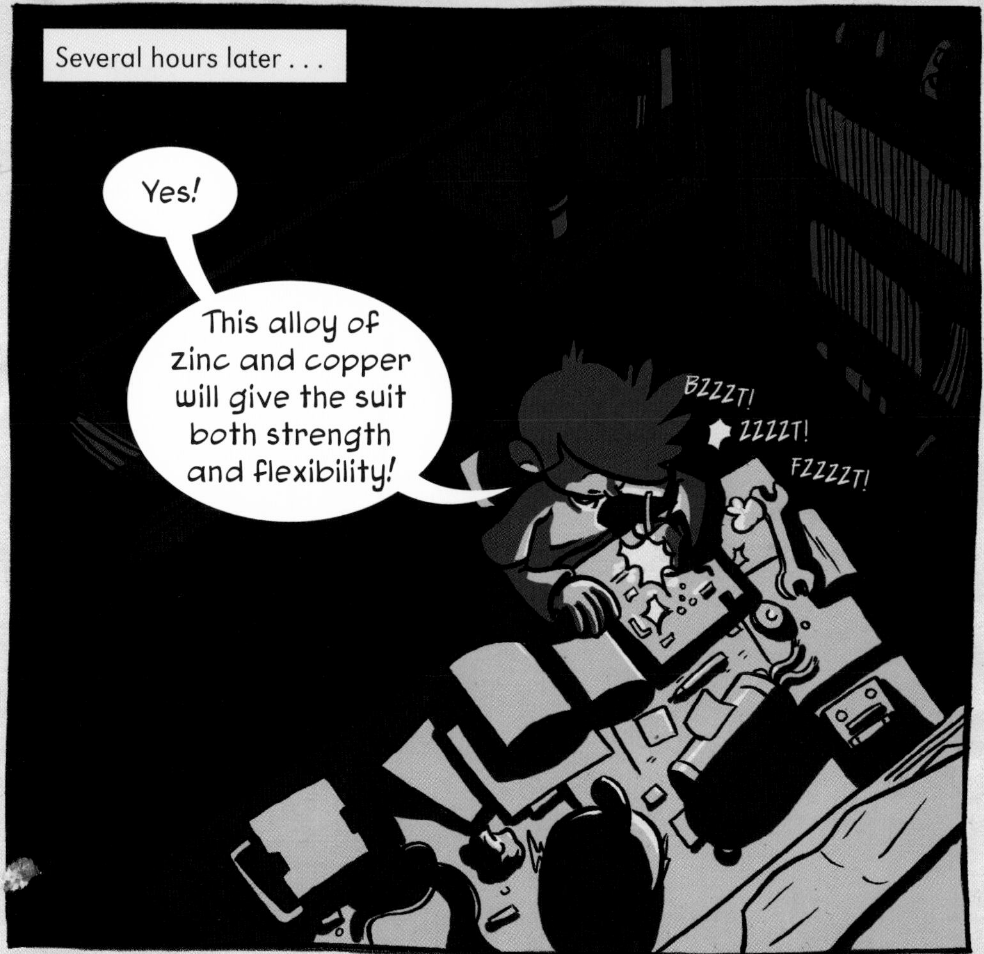
Several hours later . . .
Yes!
This alloy of zinc and copper will give the suit both strength and flexibility!
BZZZT!
ZZZZT!
FZZZZT!

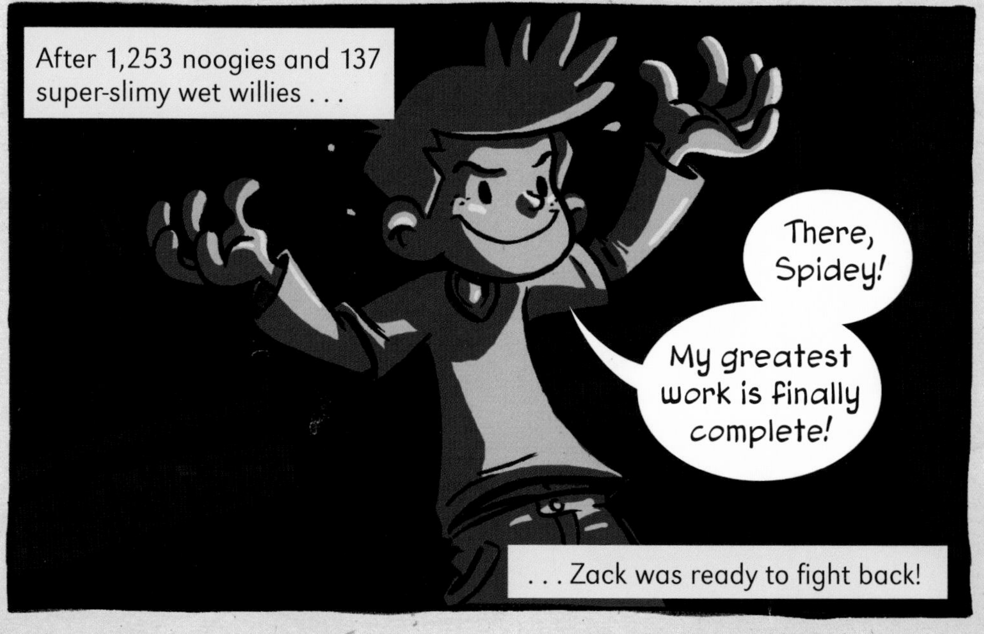
After 1,253 noogies and 137 super-slimy wet willies . . .
There, Spidey!
My greatest work is finally complete!
. . . Zack was ready to fight back!

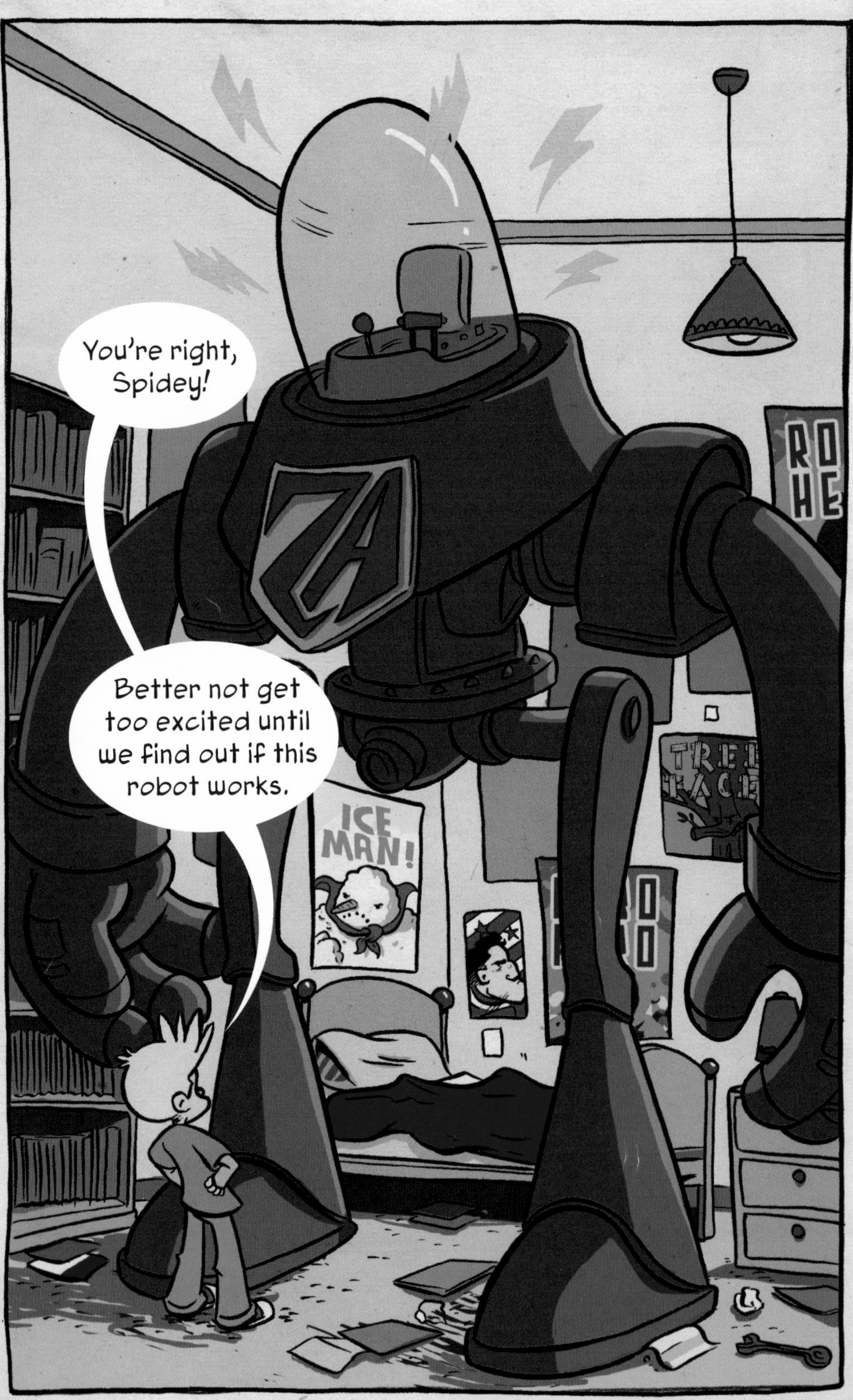
You're right, Spidey!
Better not get too excited until we find out if this robot works.
ICE MAN!

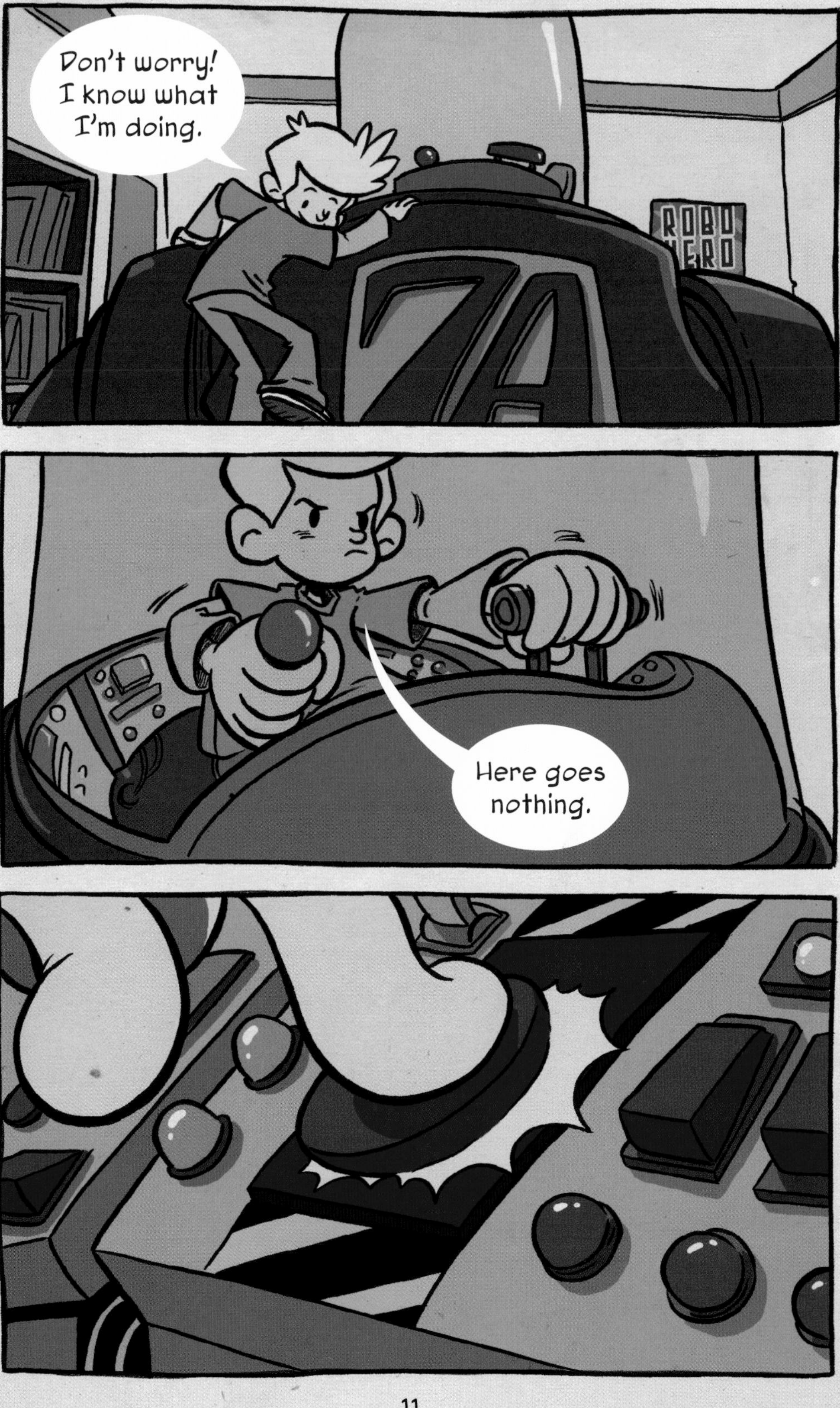
Don't worry! I know what I'm doing.
ROBO HERO
Here goes nothing.

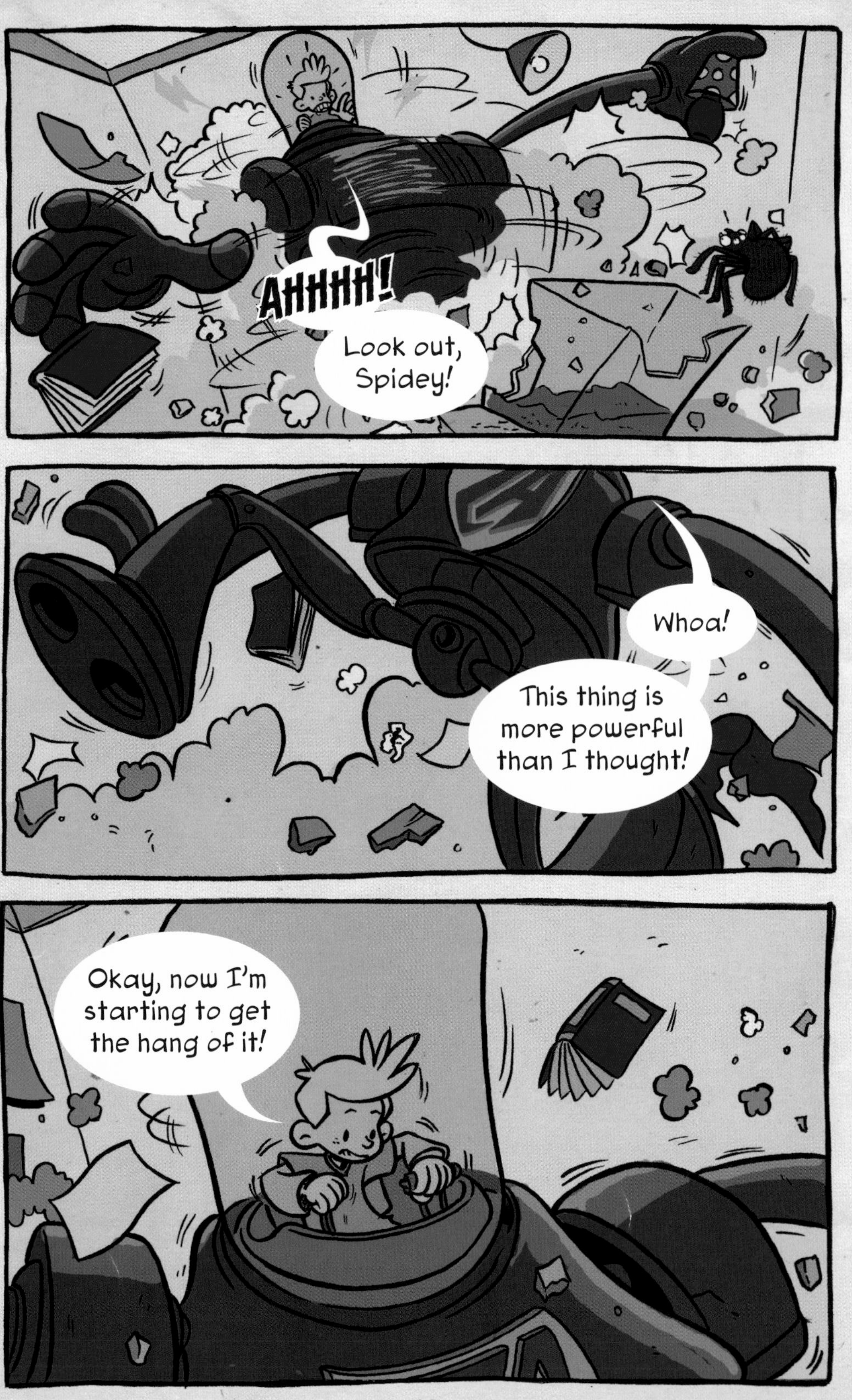
AHHHH!
Look out, Spidey!
Whoa!
This thing is more powerful than I thought!
Okay, now I'm starting to get the hang of it!

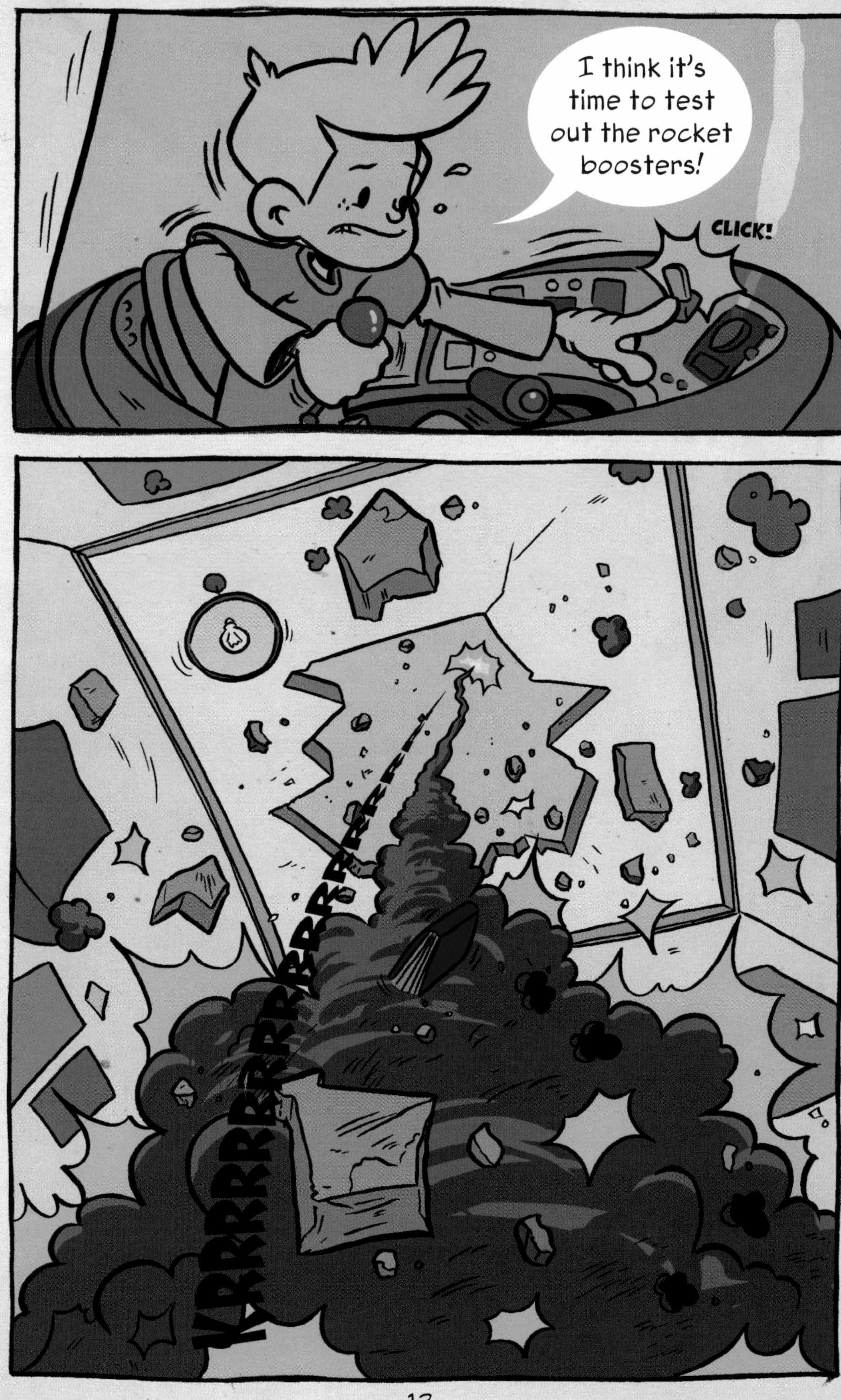
I think it's time to test out the rocket boosters!
CLICK!
KRRRRRRRRRRRRR

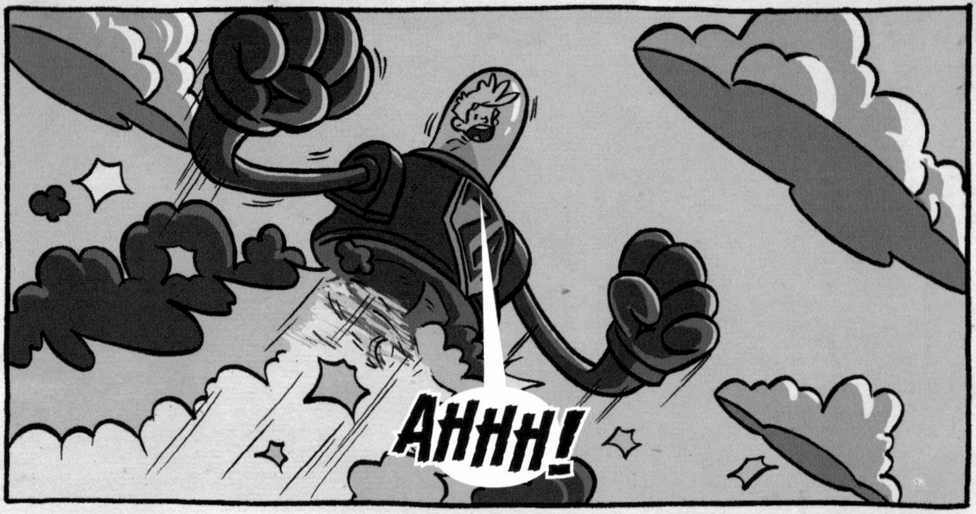
AHHH!

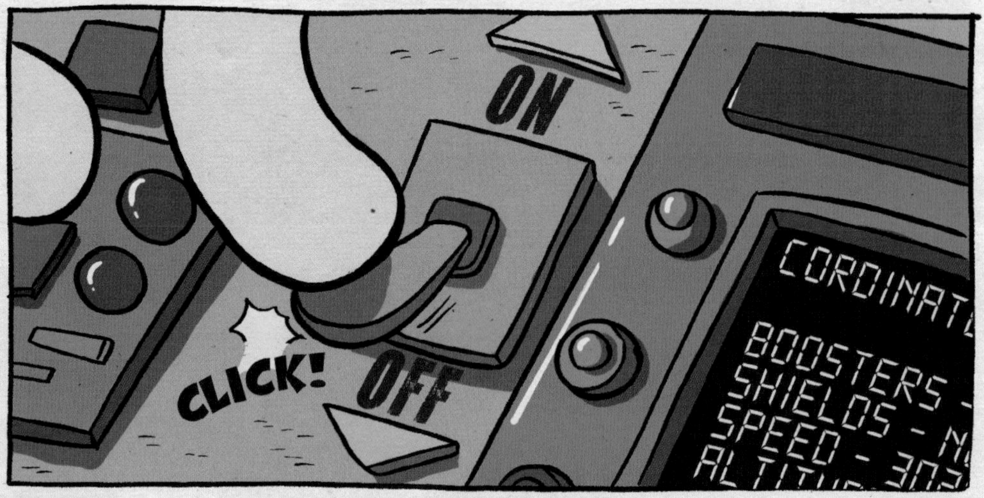
ON
CLICK!
OFF
BOOSTERS -
SHIELDS -
SPEED -

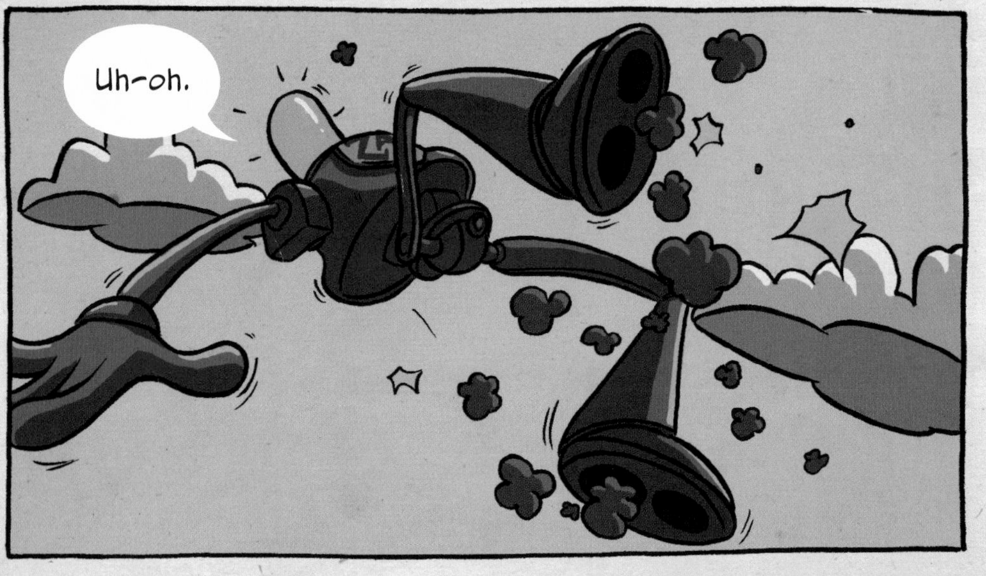
Uh-oh.

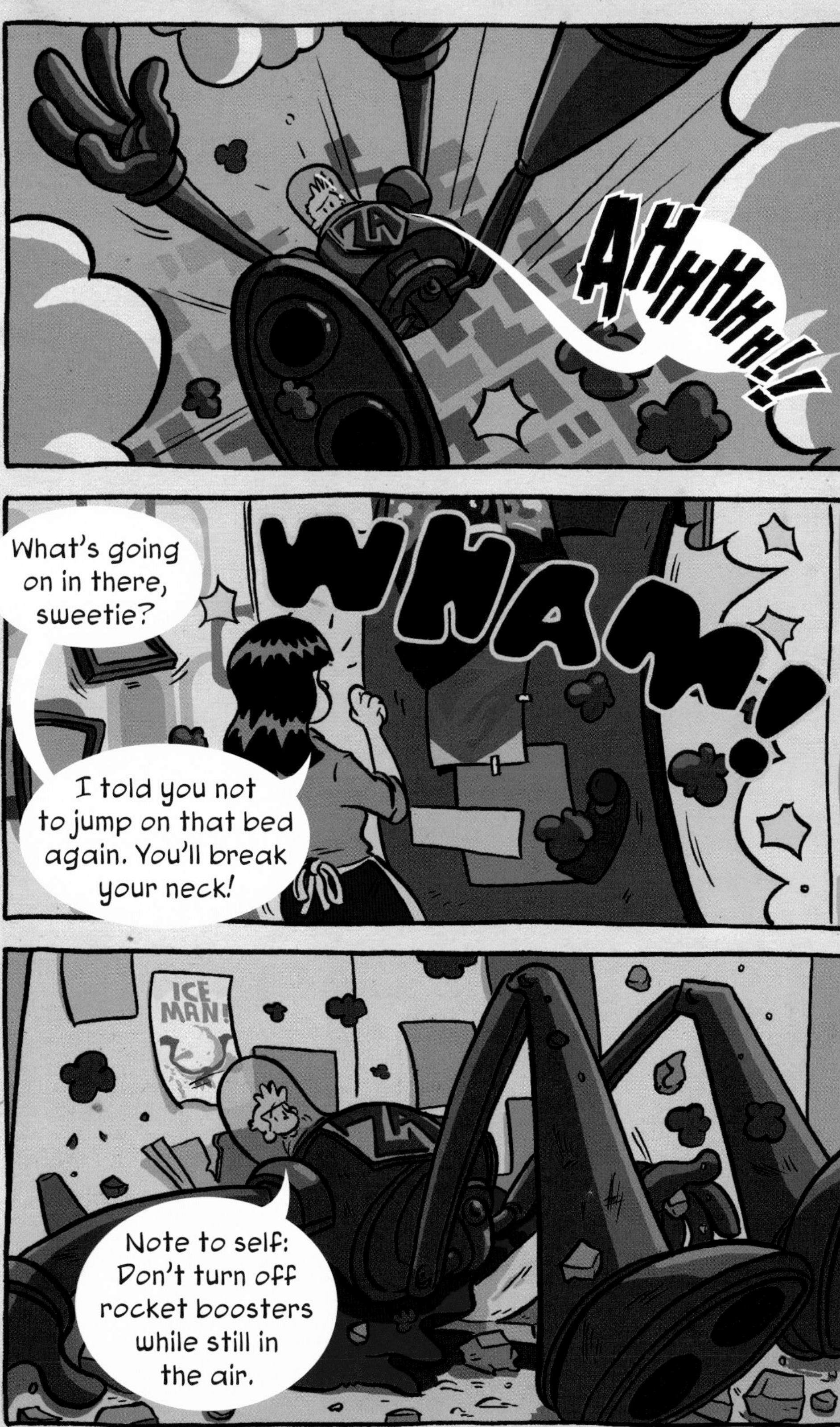
AHHHHH!!!
What's going on in there, sweetie?
WHAM!
I told you not to jump on that bed again. You'll break your neck!
ICE MAN!
Note to self: Don't turn off rocket boosters while still in the air.

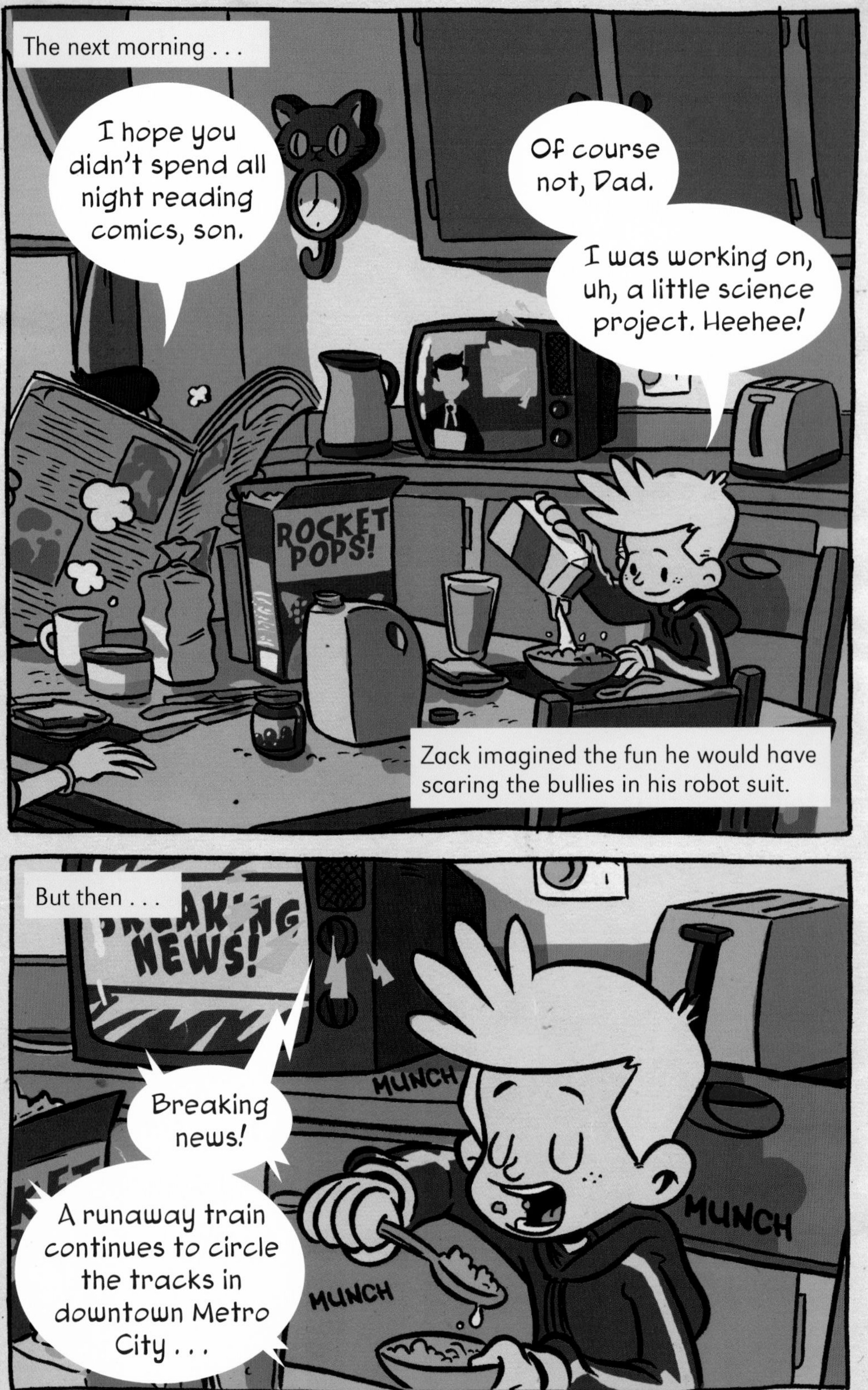
The next morning . . .
I hope you didn't spend all night reading comics, son.
Of course not, Dad.
I was working on, uh, a little science project. Heehee!
ROCKET POPS!
Zack imagined the fun he would have scaring the bullies in his robot suit.
But then . . .
NEWS!
MUNCH
Breaking news!
A runaway train continues to circle the tracks in downtown Metro City . . .
MUNCH
MUNCH

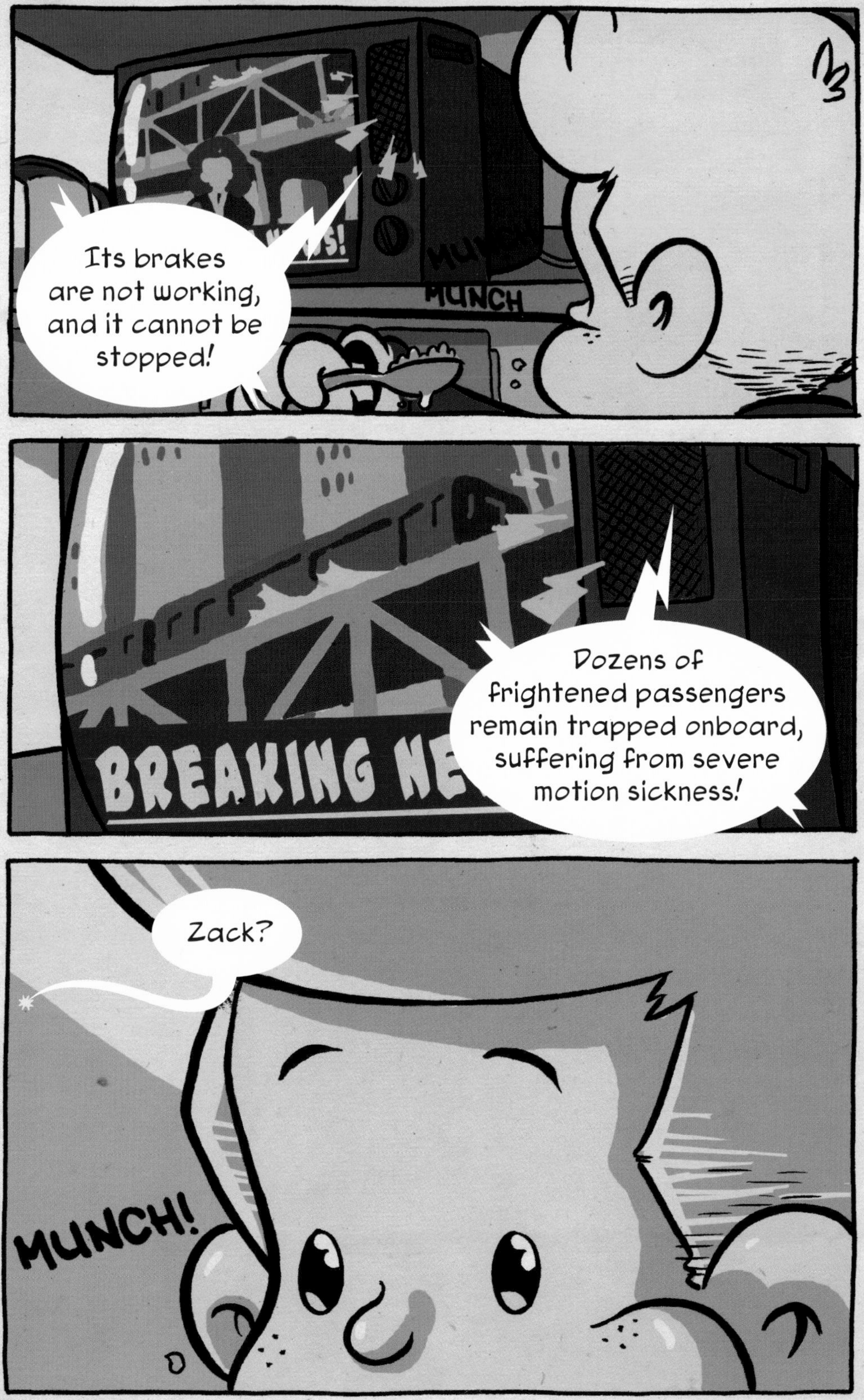
Its brakes are not working, and it cannot be stopped!
MUNCH
BREAKING
Dozens of frightened passengers remain trapped onboard, suffering from severe motion sickness!
Zack?
MUNCH!

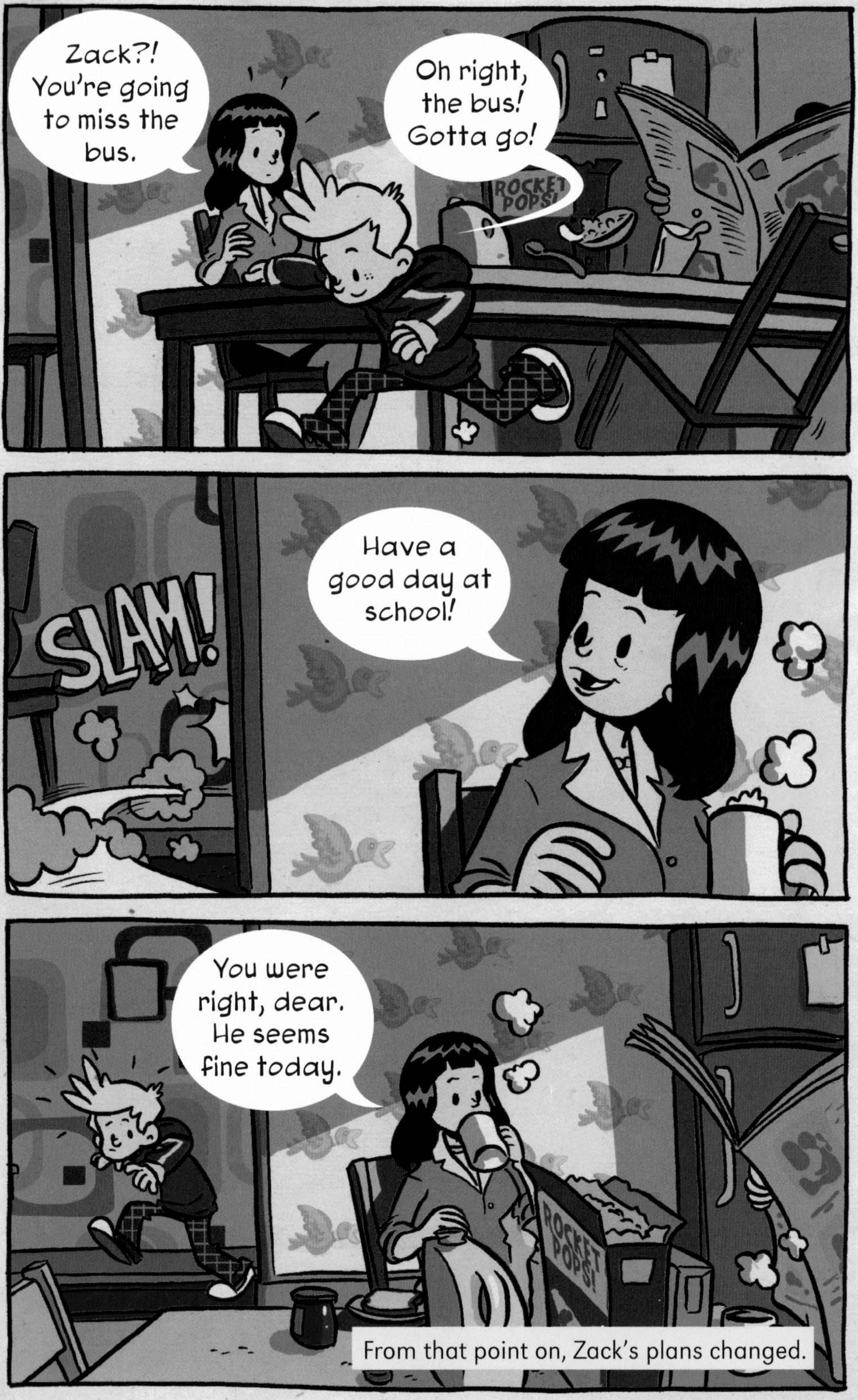
Zack?! You're going to miss the bus.
Oh right, the bus! Gotta go!
ROCKET POPS!
SLAM!
Have a good day at school!
You were right, dear. He seems fine today.
ROCKET POPS!
From that point on, Zack's plans changed.

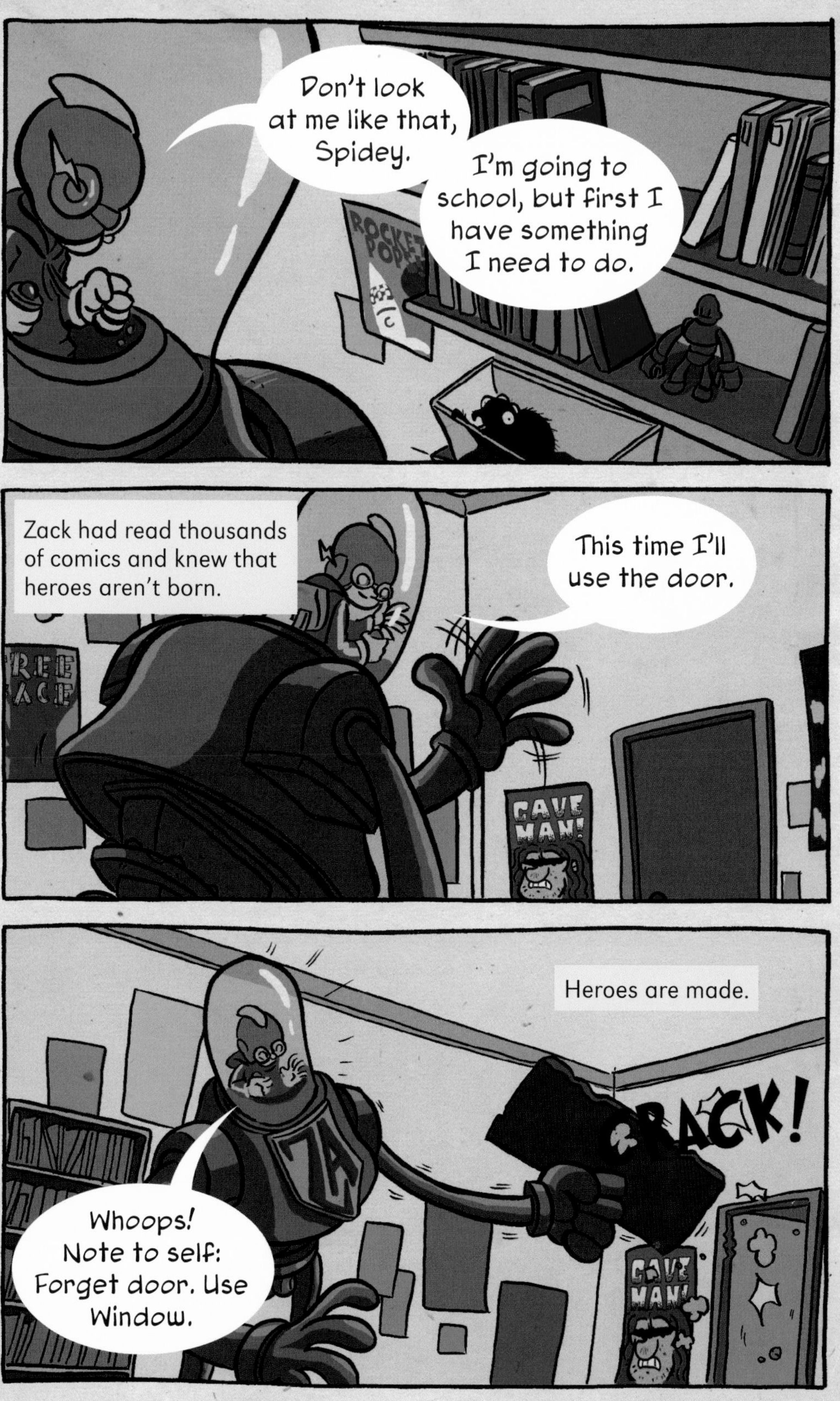
Don't look at me like that, Spidey.
I'm going to school, but first I have something I need to do.
ROCKET POP
Zack had read thousands of comics and knew that heroes aren't born.
This time I'll use the door.
CAVE MAN!
Heroes are made.
ACK!
Whoops! Note to self: Forget door. Use Window.
CAVE MAN!

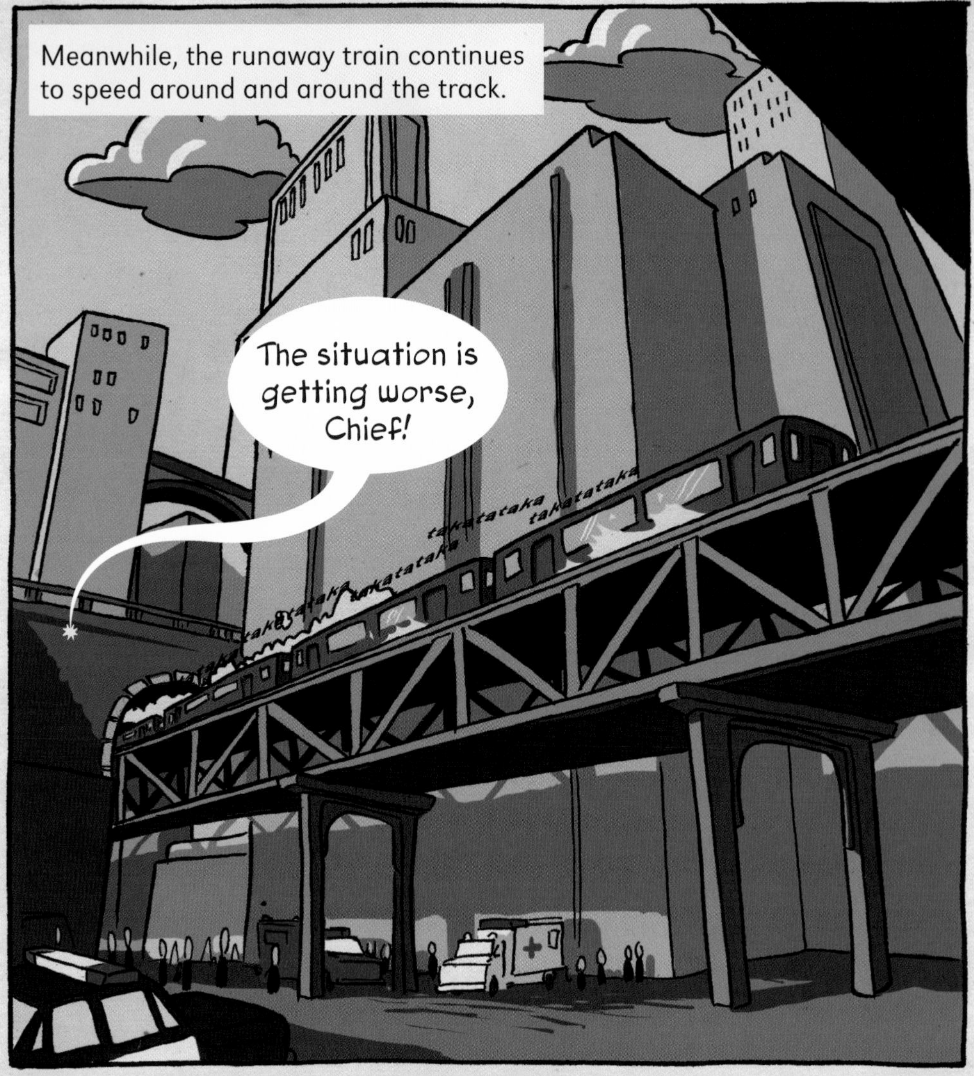
Meanwhile, the runaway train continues to speed around and around the track.
takatataka
takatataka
takatataka
takatataka
The situation is getting worse, Chief!

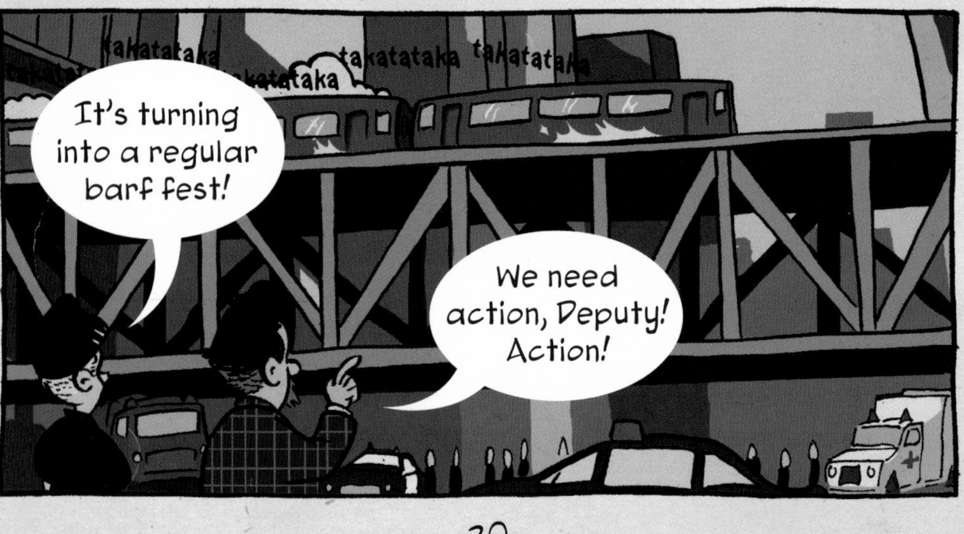
takatataka
takatataka
takatataka
takatataka
It's turning into a regular barf fest!
We need action, Deputy! Action!

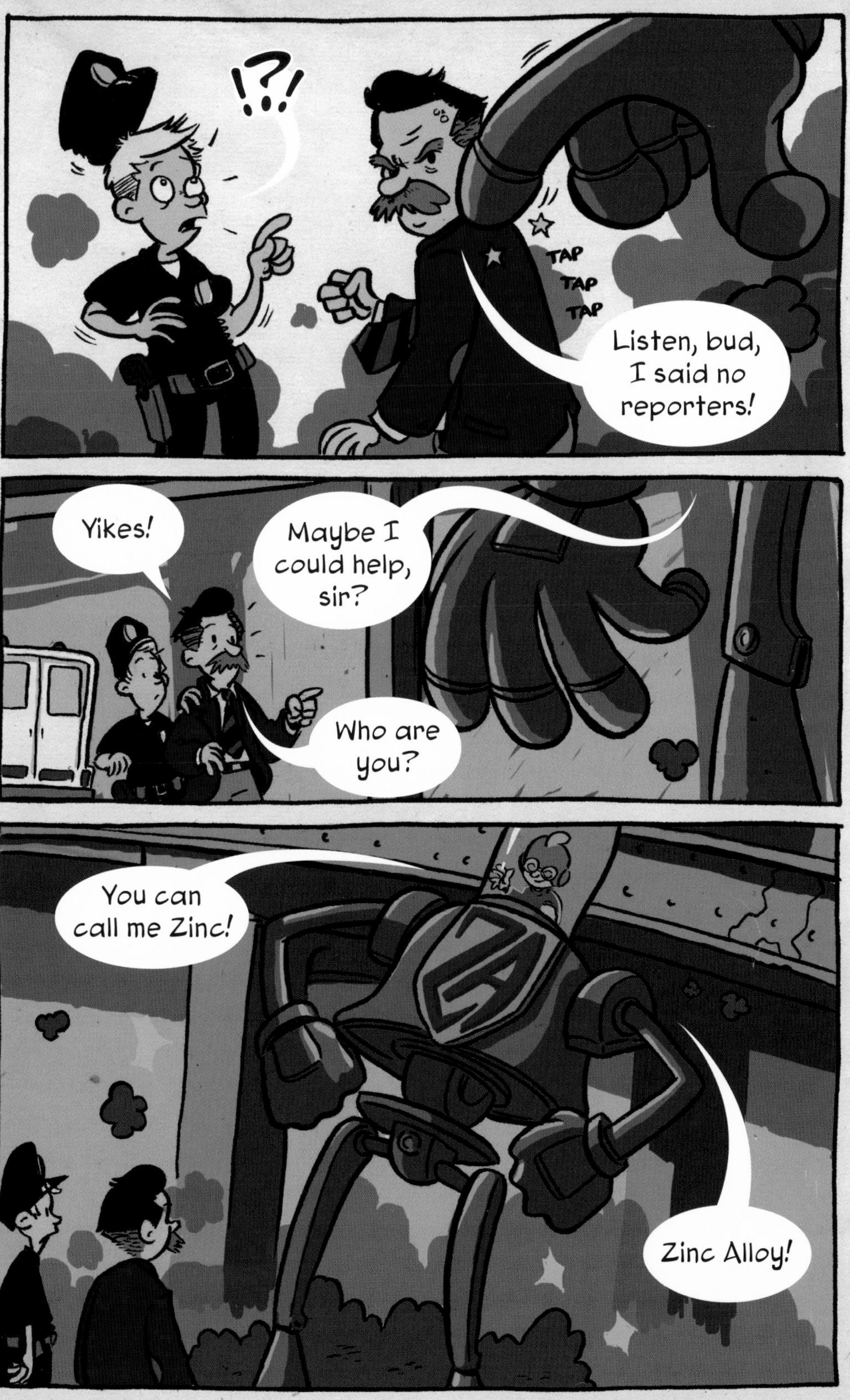
!?!
TAP
TAP
TAP
Listen, bud, I said no reporters!
Yikes!
Maybe I could help, sir?
Who are you?
You can call me Zinc!
Zinc Alloy!

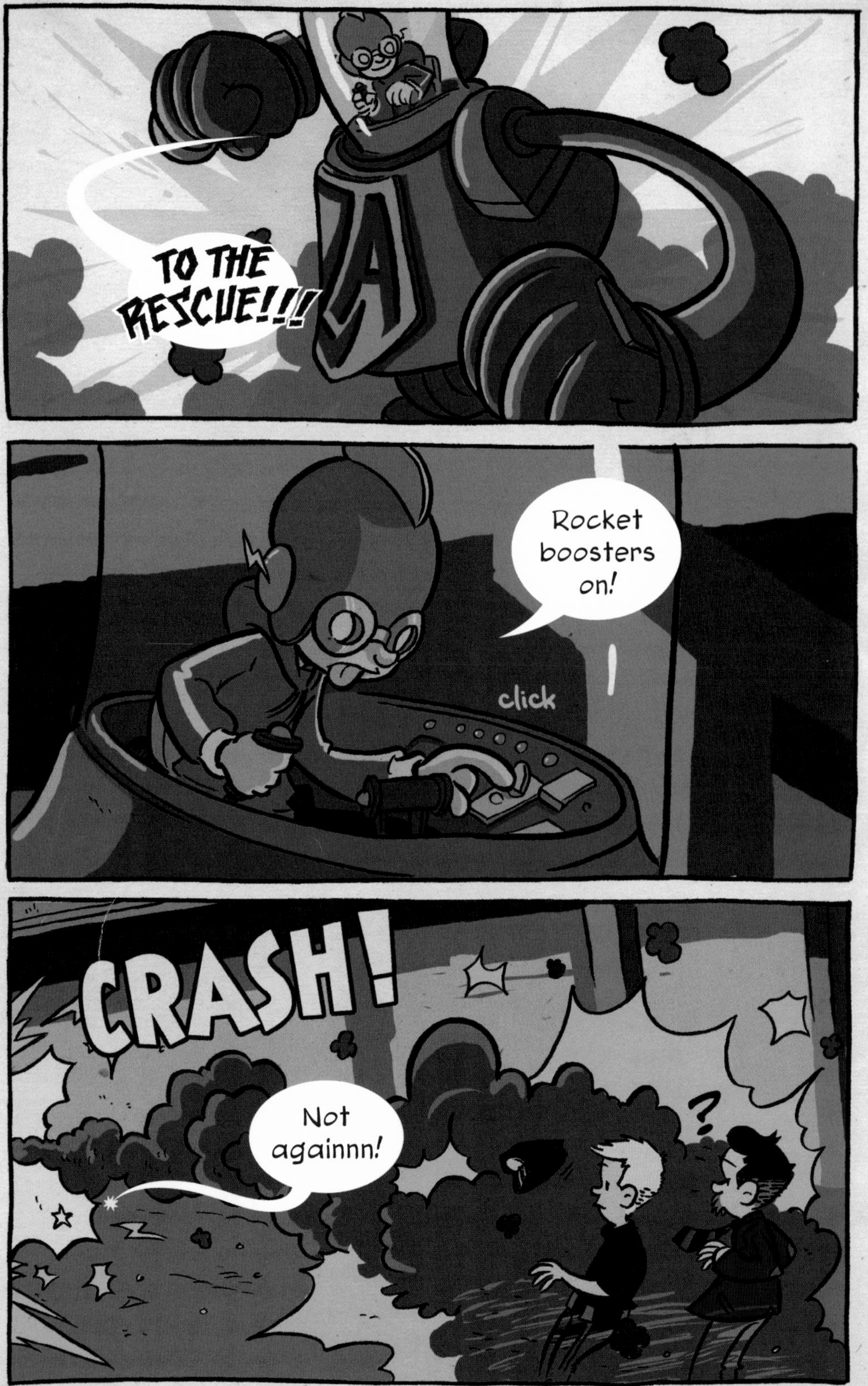
TO THE RESCUE!!!
Rocket boosters on!
click
CRASH!
Not againnn!
?

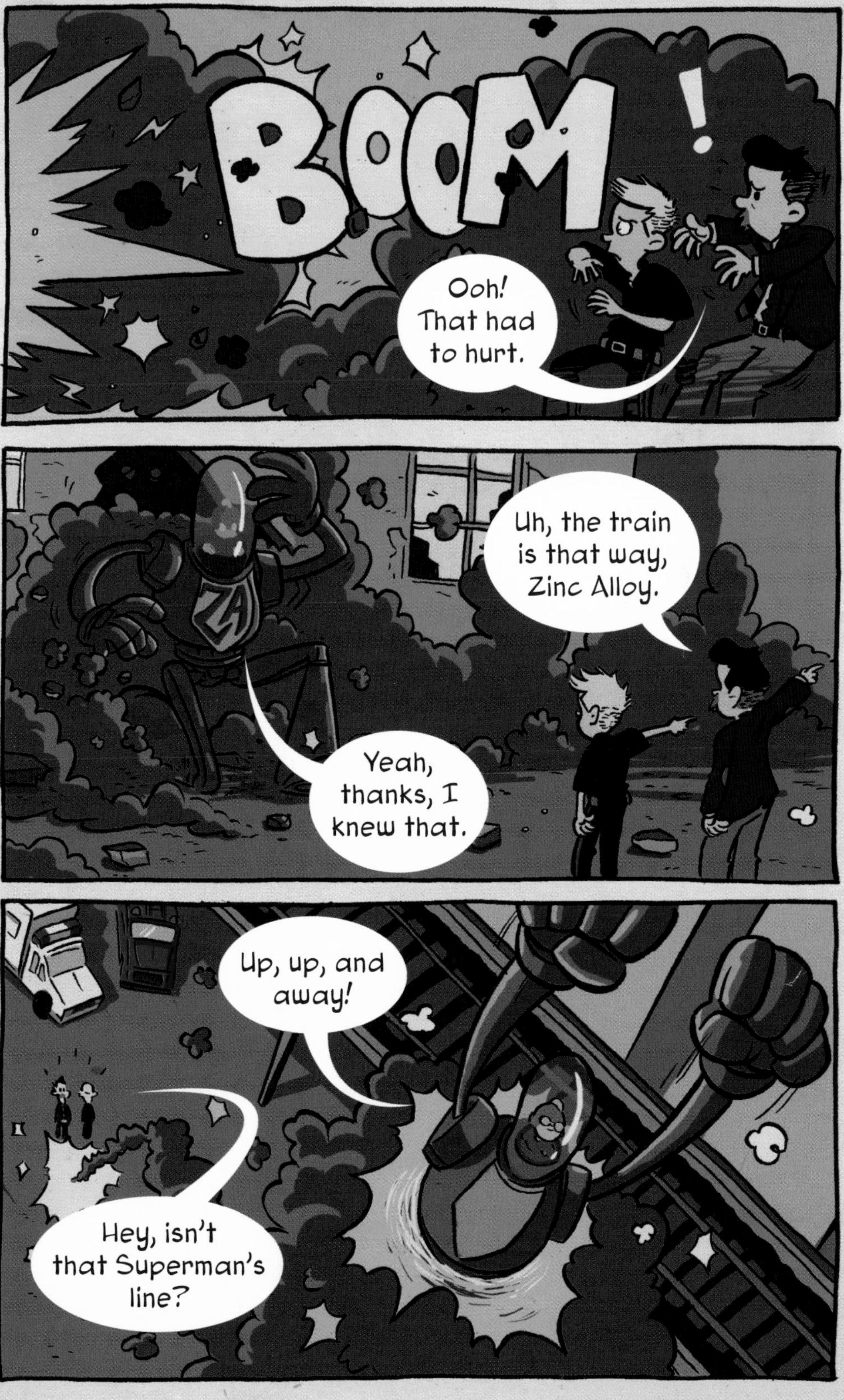
BOOM!
Ooh! That had to hurt.
Uh, the train is that way, Zinc Alloy.
Yeah, thanks, I knew that.
Up, up, and away!
Hey, isn't that Superman's line?

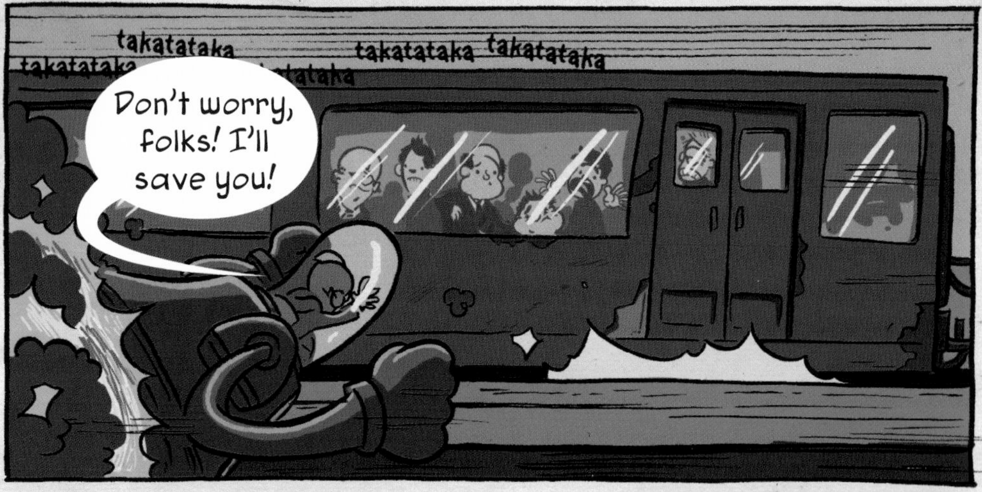
takatataka
takatataka
takatataka
takatataka takatataka
Don't worry, folks! I'll save you!

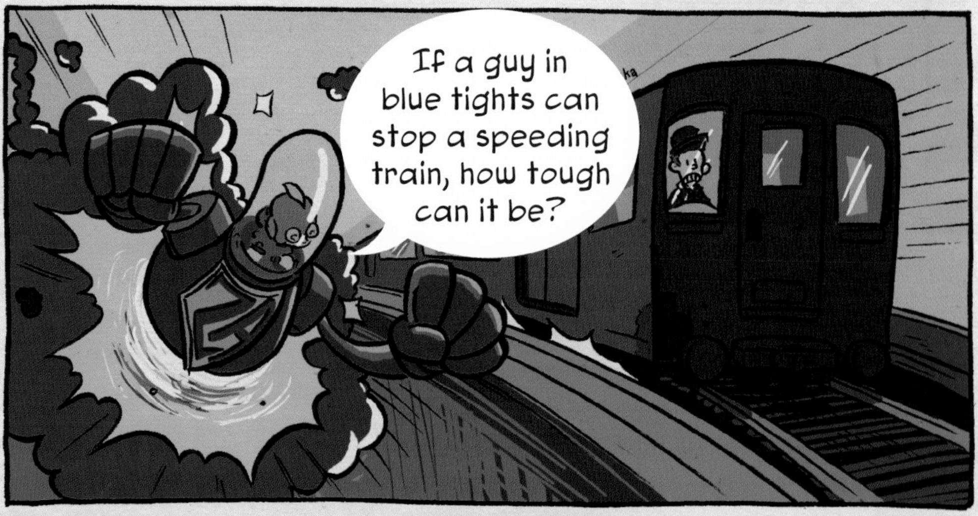
If a guy in blue tights can stop a speeding train, how tough can it be?

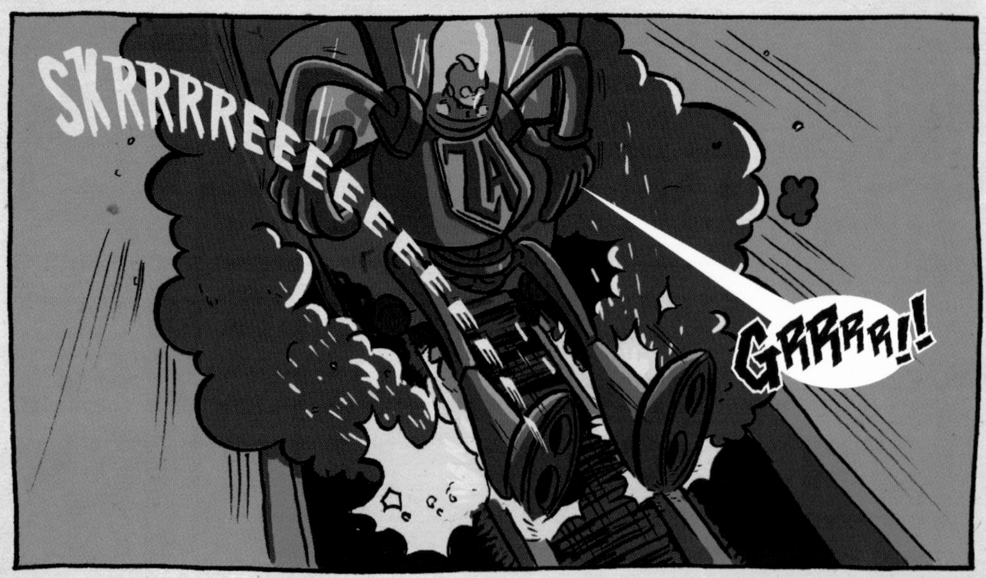
SKRRRRREEEEEEEEEE
GRRRR!!

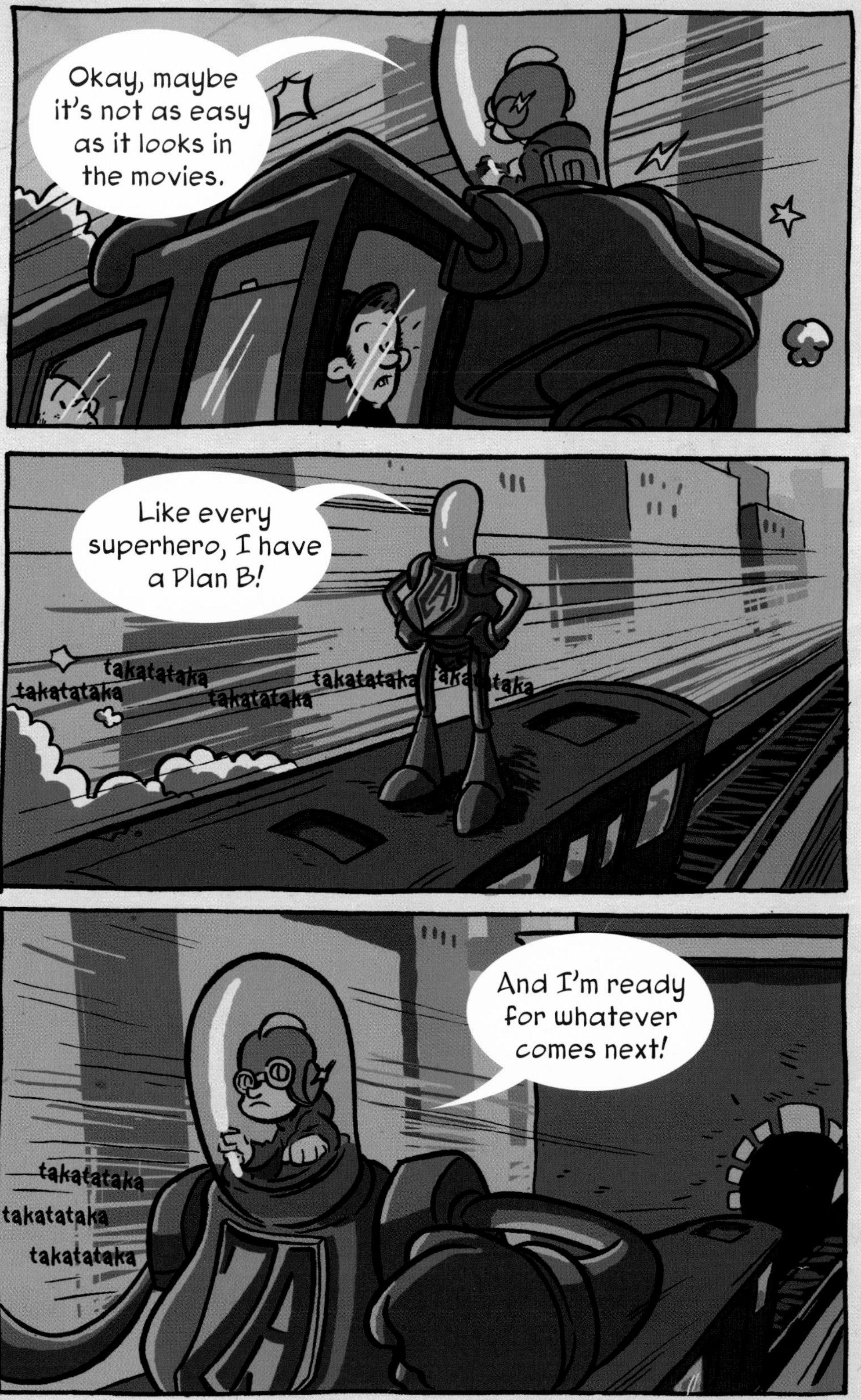
Okay, maybe it's not as easy as it looks in the movies.
Like every superhero, I have a Plan B!
takatataka
takatataka
takatataka
takatataka
takatataka
And I'm ready for whatever comes next!
takatataka
takatataka
takatataka

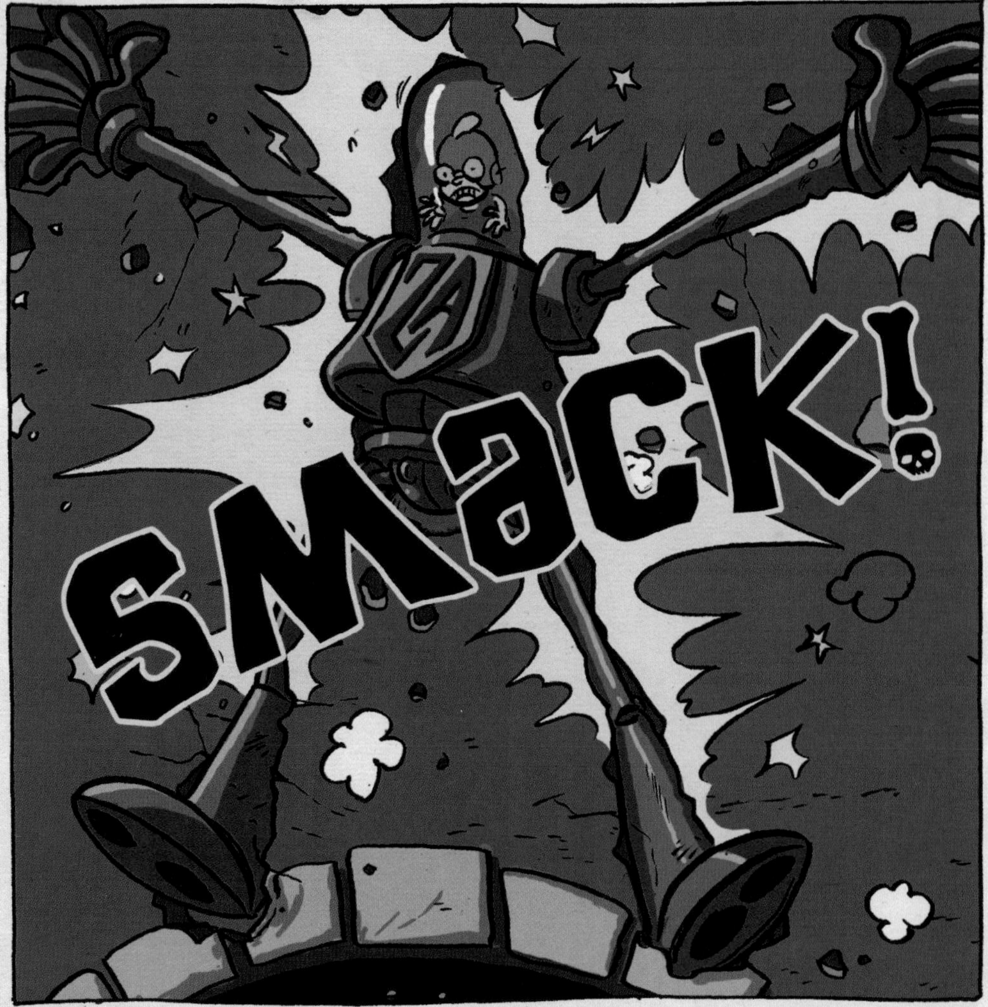
SMACK!

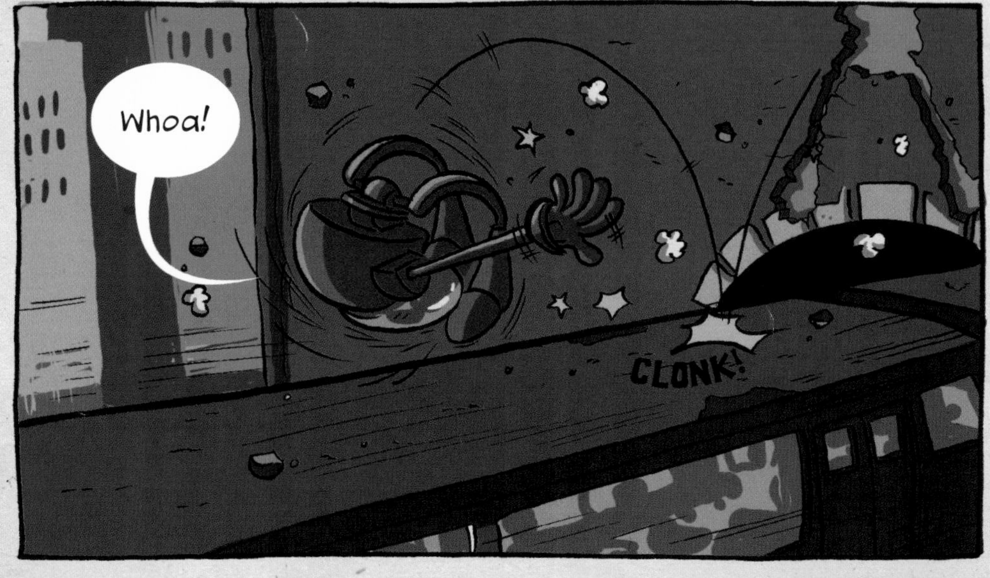
Whoa!
CLONK!

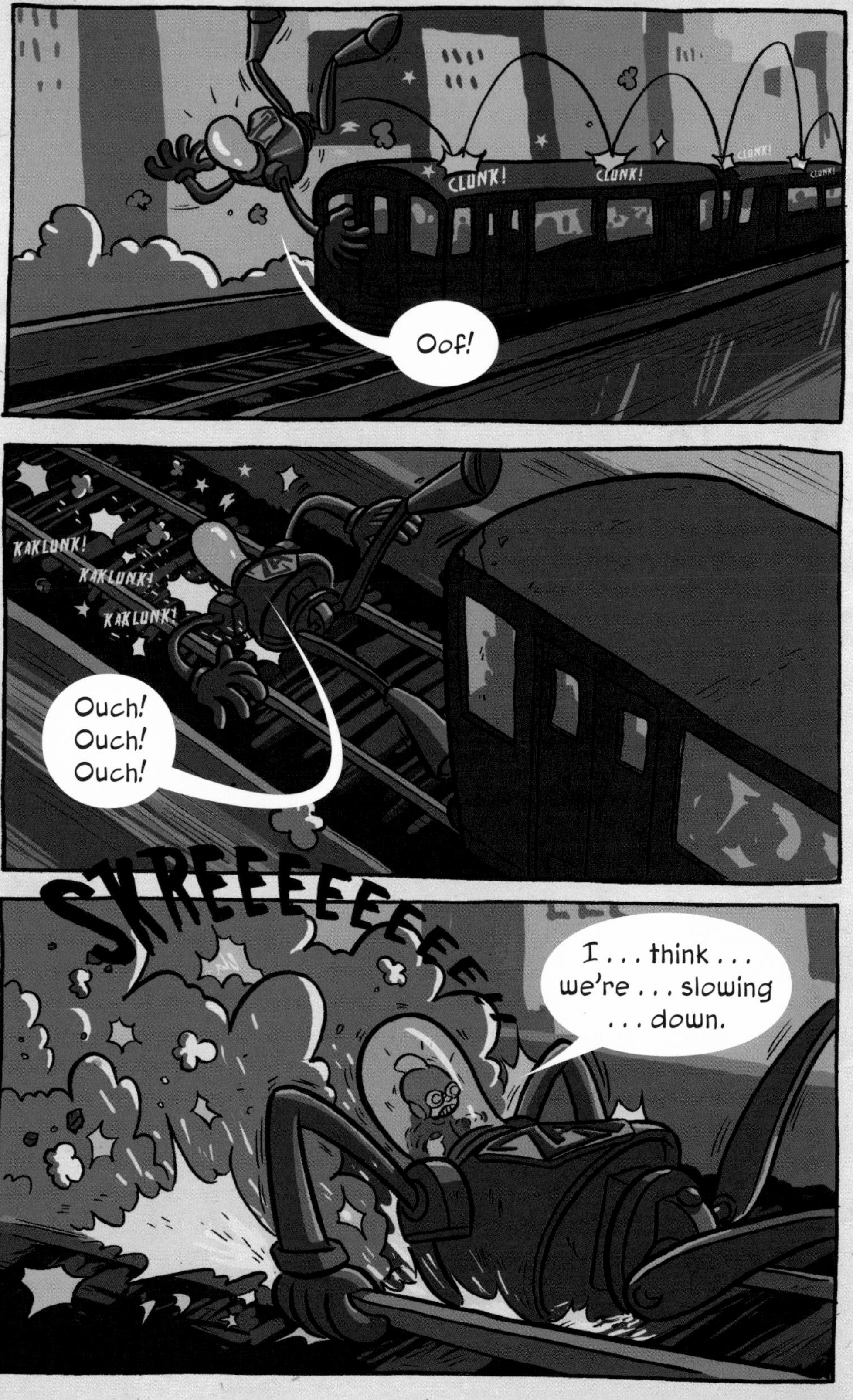

CLUNK!
CLUNK!
CLUNK!
CLUNK!
Oof!
KAKLUNK!
KAKLUNK!
KAKLUNK!
Ouch! Ouch! Ouch!
SKREEEEEEEE...
I . . . think . . . we're . . . slowing . . . down.

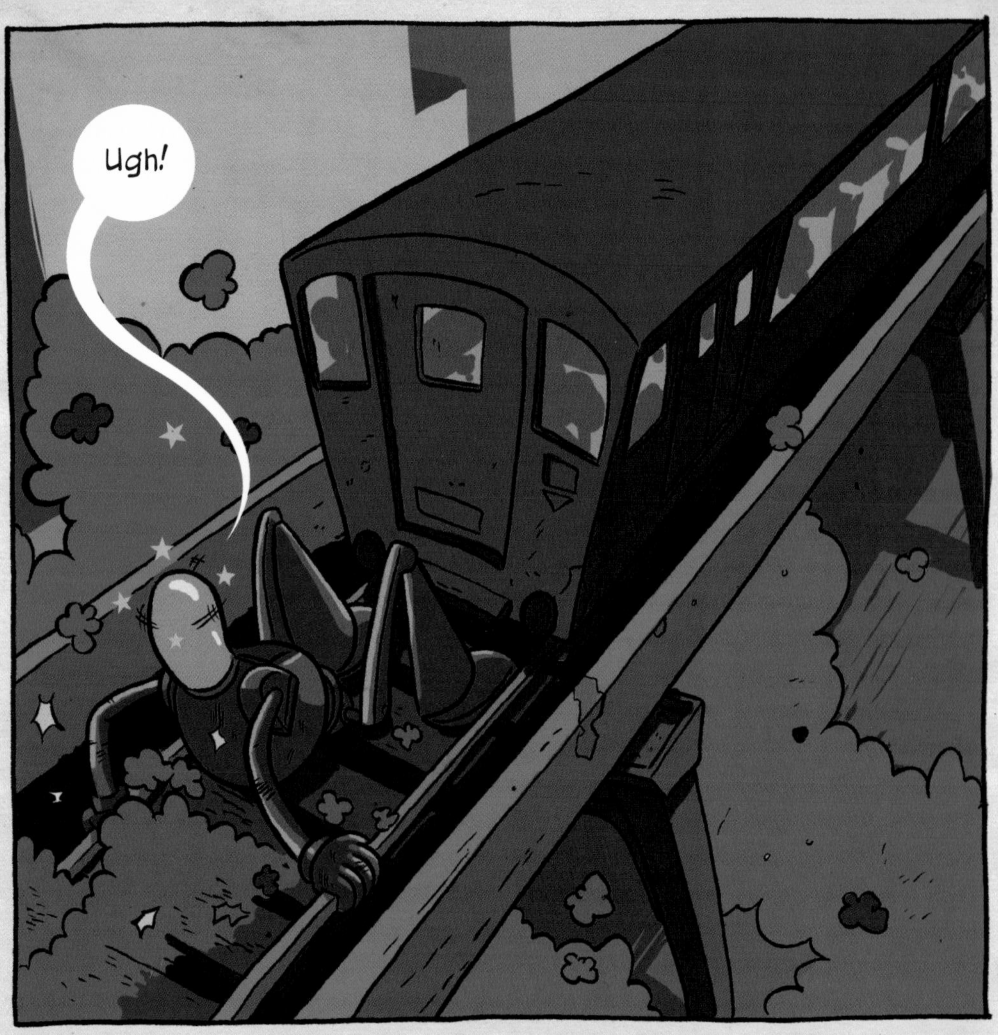
Ugh!

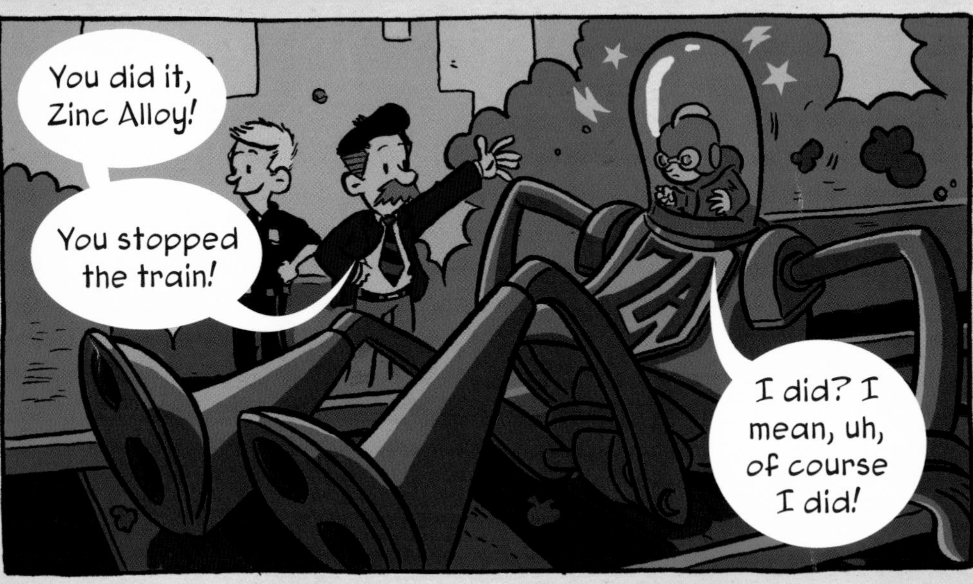
You did it, Zinc Alloy!
You stopped the train!
I did? I mean, uh, of course I did!

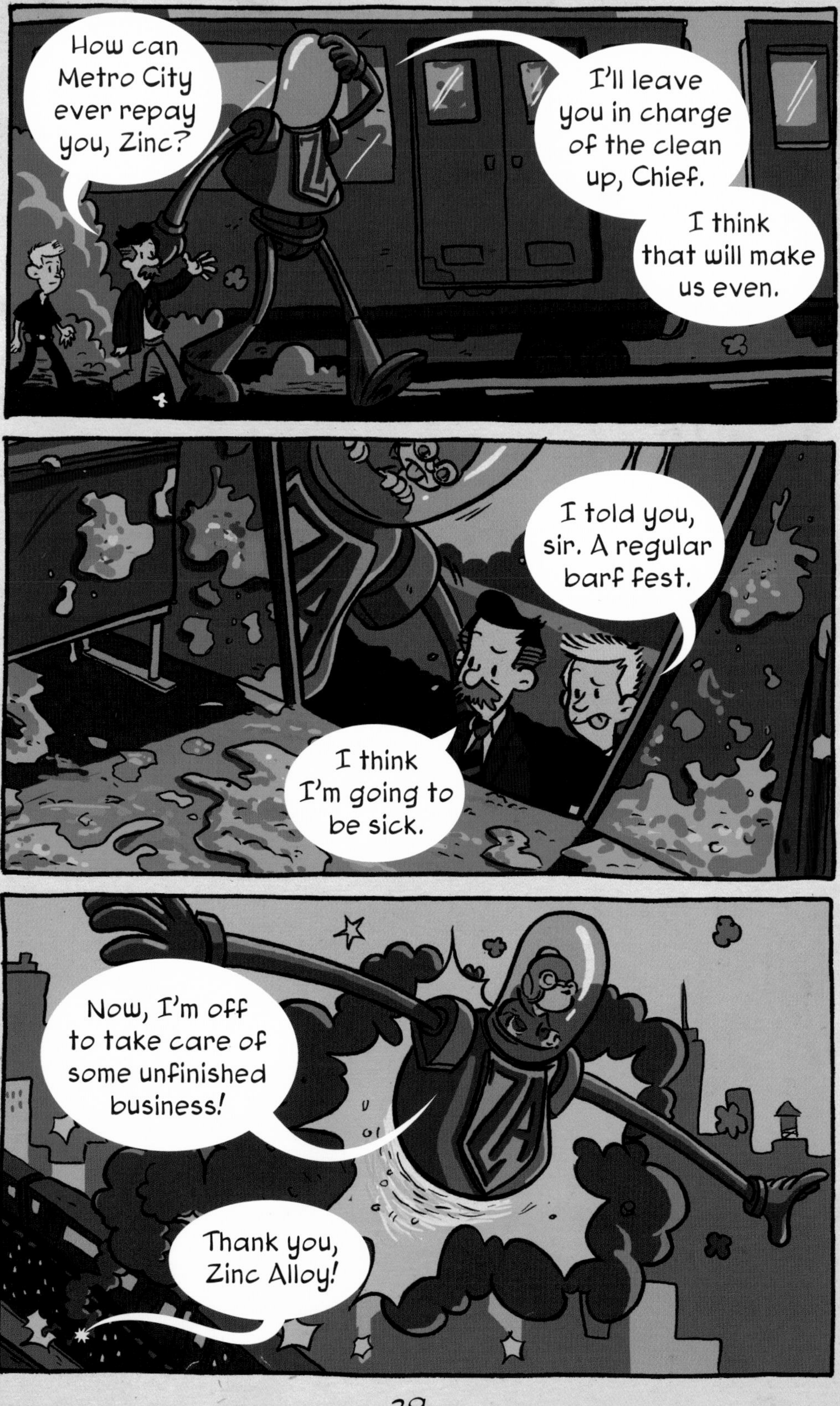
How can Metro City ever repay you, Zinc?
I'll leave you in charge of the clean up, Chief.
I think that will make us even.
I told you, sir. A regular barf fest.
I think I'm going to be sick.
Now, I'm off to take care of some unfinished business!
Thank you, Zinc Alloy!

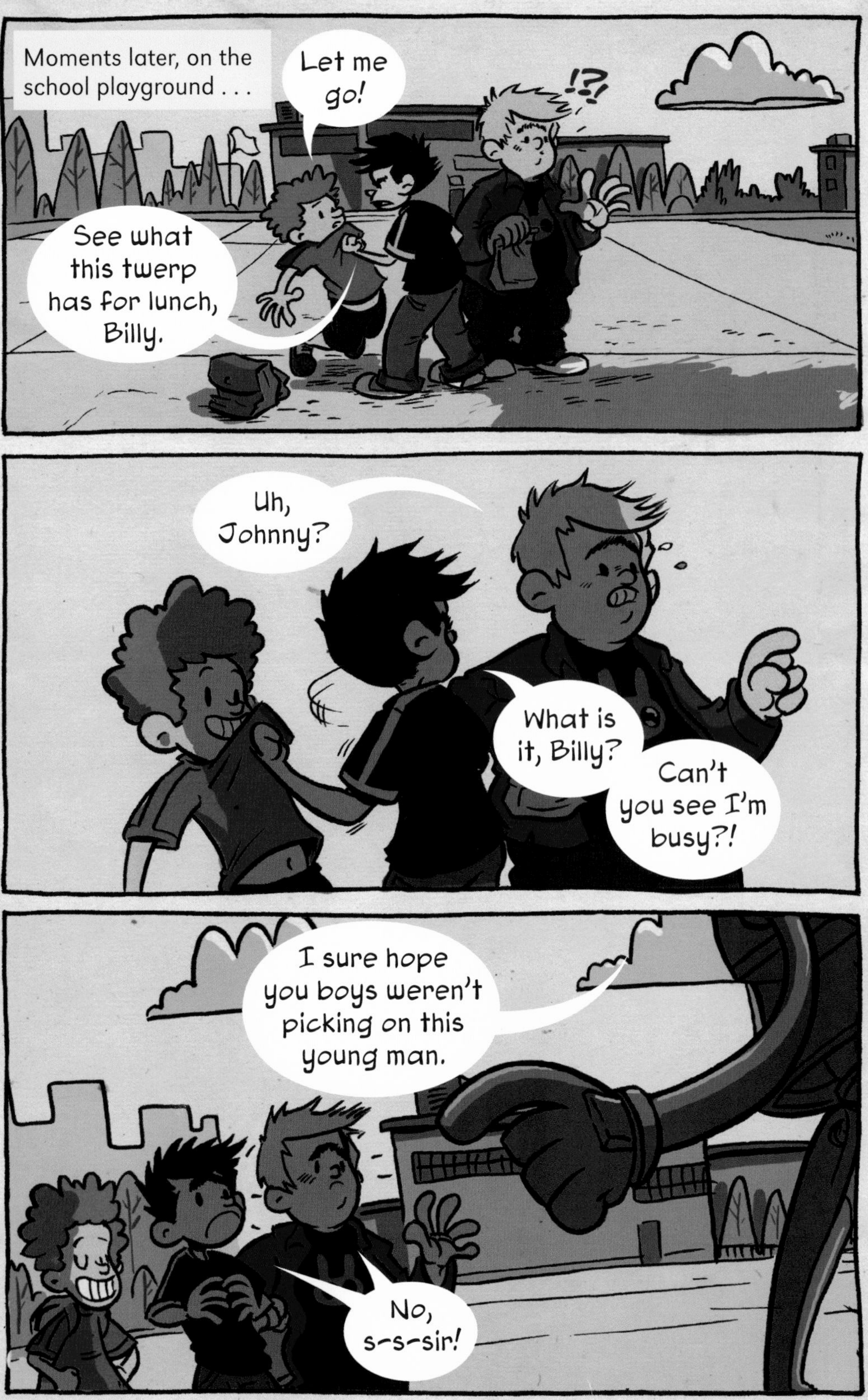
Moments later, on the school playground . . .
Let me go!
!?!
See what this twerp has for lunch, Billy.
Uh, Johnny?
What is it, Billy?
Can't you see I'm busy?!
I sure hope you boys weren't picking on this young man.
No, s-s-sir!

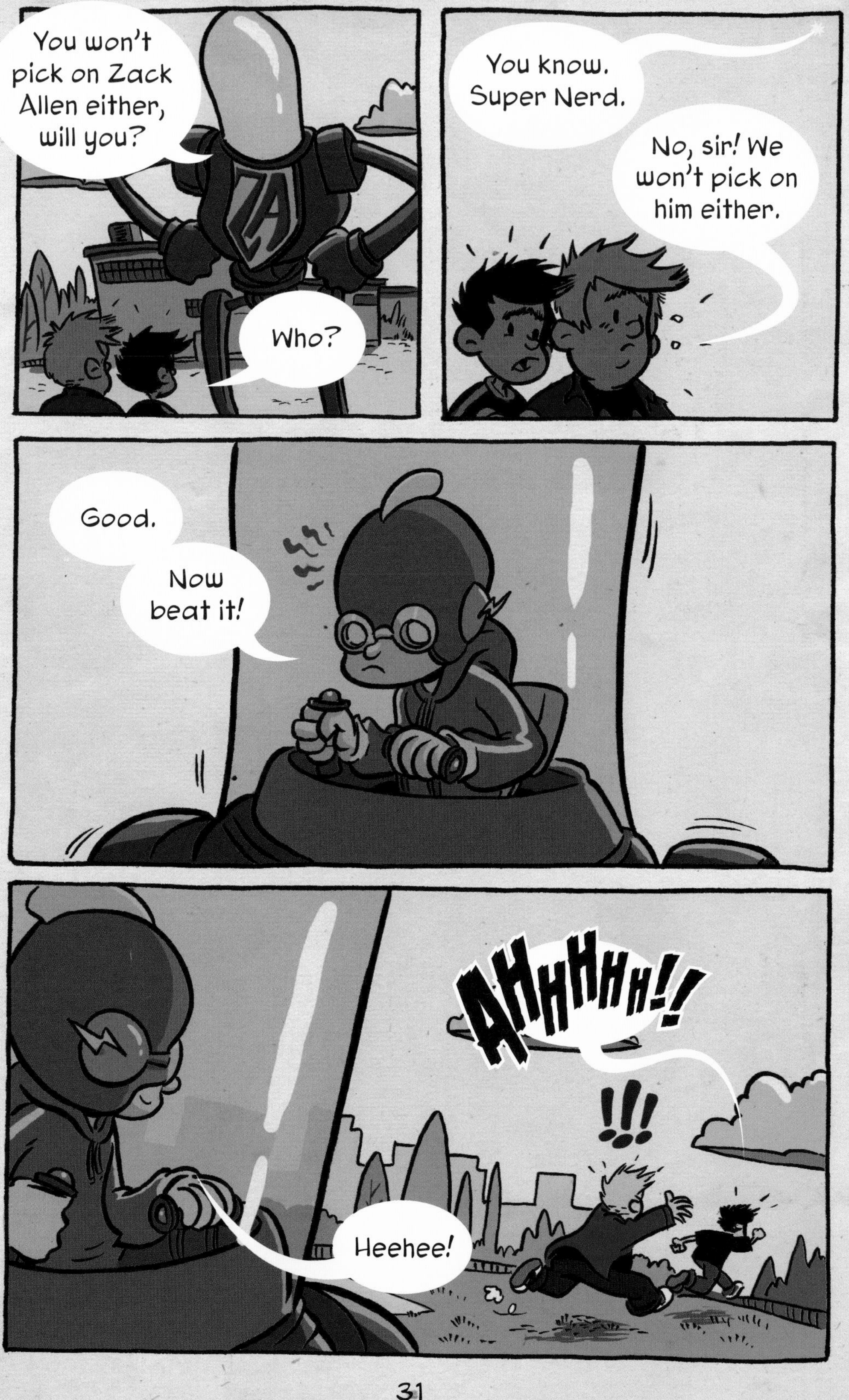

You won't pick on Zack Allen either, will you?
Who?
You know. Super Nerd.
No, sir! We won't pick on him either.
Good.
Now beat it!
AHHHHH!!
!!!
Heehee!

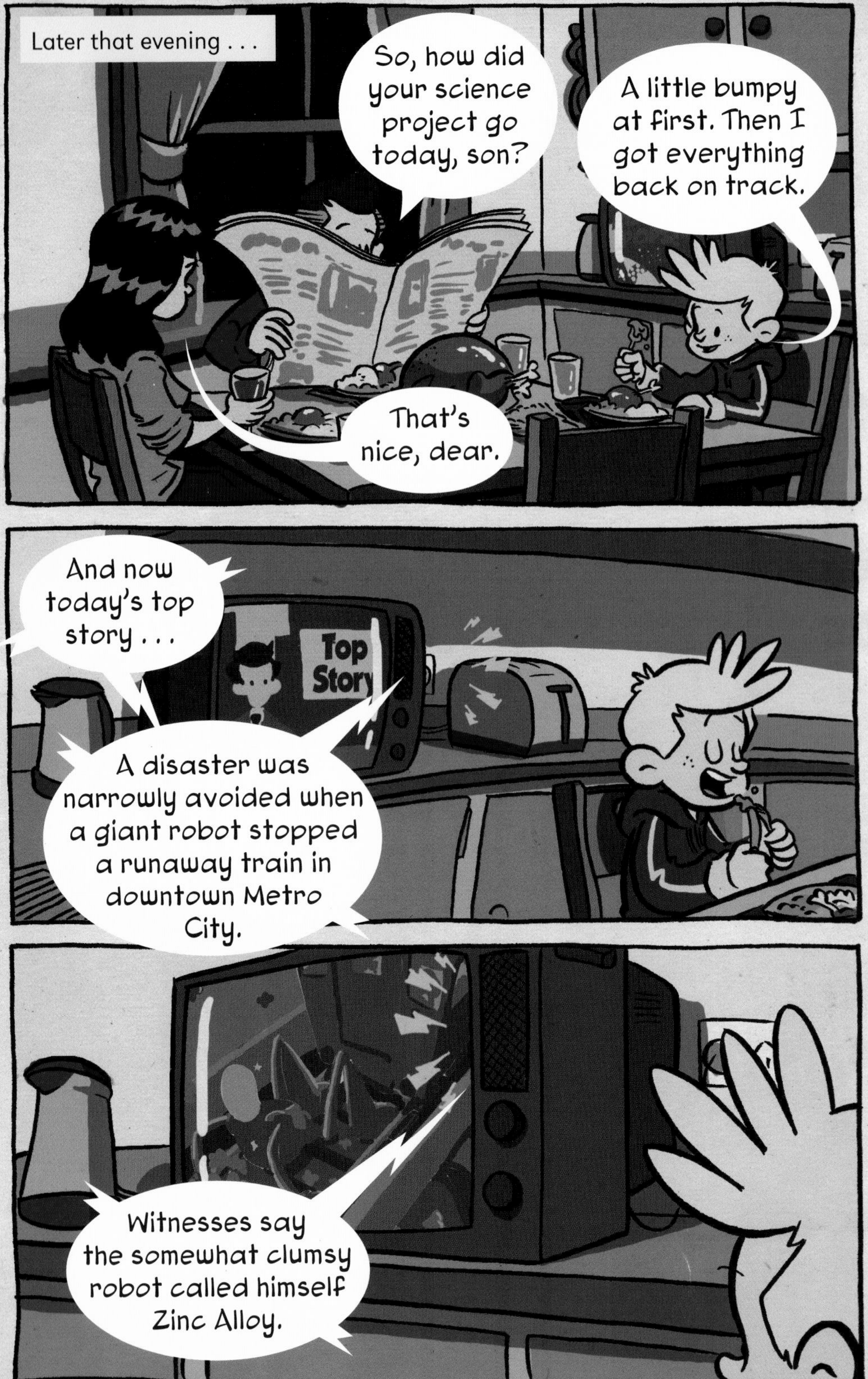
Later that evening . . .
So, how did your science project go today, son?
A little bumpy at first. Then I got everything back on track.
That's nice, dear.
And now today's top story . . .
Top Story
A disaster was narrowly avoided when a giant robot stopped a runaway train in downtown Metro City.
Witnesses say the somewhat clumsy robot called himself Zinc Alloy.

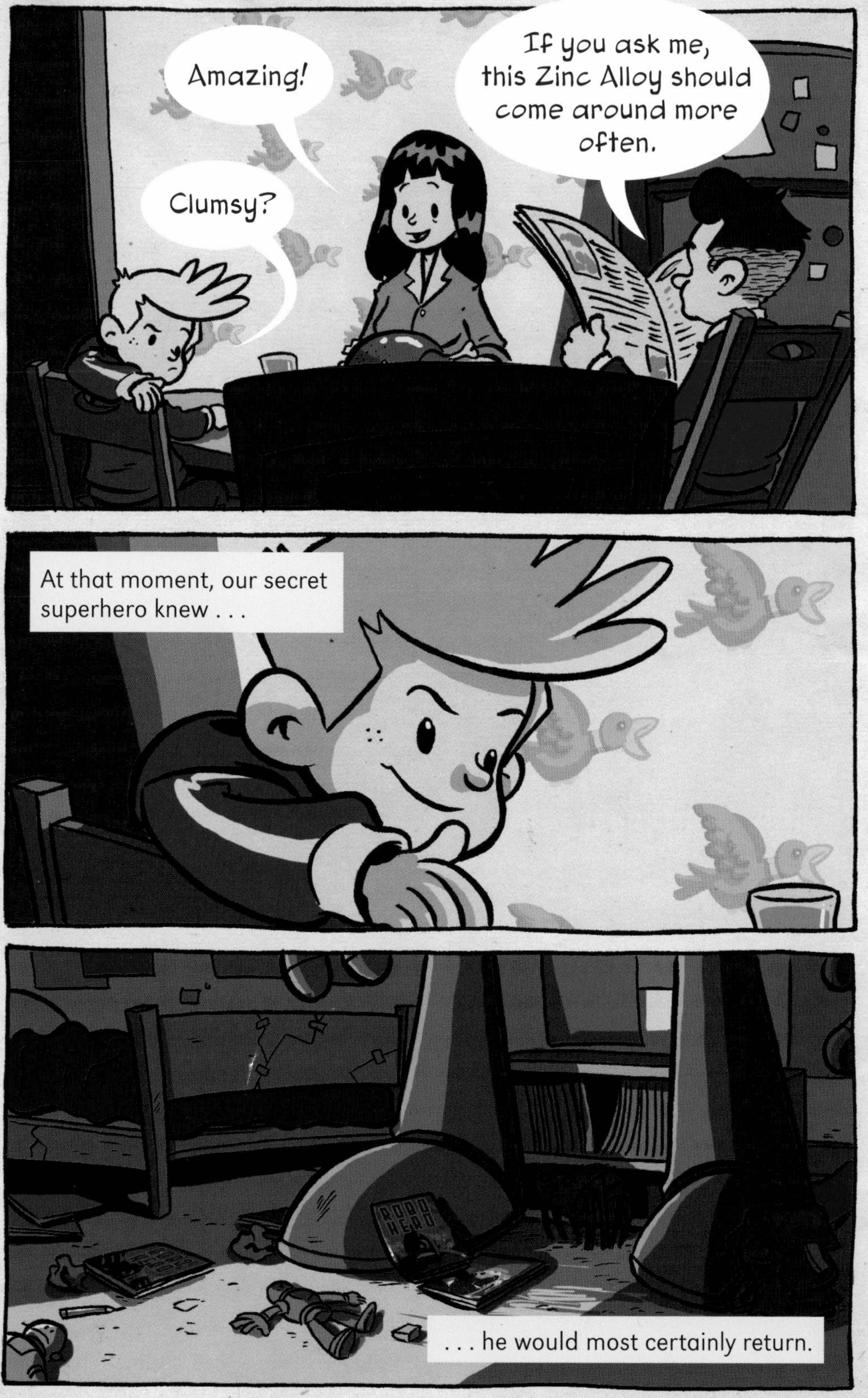
Amazing!
Clumsy?
If you ask me, this Zinc Alloy should come around more often.
At that moment, our secret superhero knew . . .
. . . he would most certainly return.

About the Author

Growing up in a small Minnesota town, Donald Lemke kept himself busy reading anything from comic books to classic novels. Today, Lemke works as a children's book editor and pursues a master's degree in publishing from Hamline University in St. Paul, Minnesota. Lemke has written a variety of children's books and graphic novels. His ideas often come to him while running along the inspiring trails near his home.

About the Illustrator

Douglas Holgate is a freelance illustrator from Melbourne, Australia. His work has been published all around the world by Random House, Simon and Schuster, the *New Yorker* magazine, and Image Comics. His award-winning comic "Laika" appears in the acclaimed comic collection *Flight, Volume Two*.

Glossary

alloy (AL-oi)—a mixture of two or more types of metal

clumsy (KLUHM-zee)—careless or awkward in the way a person walks or moves

construct (kuhn-STRUHKT)—to make or build something

flexibility (flek-suh-BIL-ih-tee)—the ability to bend and change shape

noogie (NOO-gee)—rubbing one's knuckles on a person's head for a slightly painful form of torture

revealed (ri-VEE-uhld)—to make something known, such as telling a secret

rocket booster (ROK-it BOO-stur)—a special rocket that gives extra power to a spacecraft

wet willie (WET WIHL-ee)—to lick one's finger and then shove it into another person's ear

zinc (ZINGK)—a blue-white metal used in many alloys; iron and steel are often coated with zinc to keep them from rusting

History of COMICS

Did you know the first comics are more than 30,000 years old? That's right! In Lascaux, France, early humans carved and painted images of animals onto cave walls. Many people believe these are the first "comic" stories.

About 5,000 years ago ancient Egyptians used pictures and symbols, called hieroglyphs (HYE-ur-uh-glifs), to tell stories about their people and culture. Many of these tales can still be seen on the walls of Egypt's pyramids.

In 1754, Benjamin Franklin created the first cartoon published in an American newspaper. The cartoon showed a snake cut into eight pieces with the words "Join, or Die." Instead of being funny, Franklin hoped the comic would help unite the eight American colonies.

In 1897, R. F. Outcault created "The Yellow Kid," which many believe is the first comic strip. In the strip, Outcault used the first ever word balloon. Word balloons are the bubbles filled with the text of a character's spoken words.

In the early 1900s, comics and cartoons became more popular with children. In November 1928, Walt Disney released a short animated film called "Steamboat Willie." It was the first Mickey Mouse cartoon to have sound.

The first issue of *Action Comics* was released in June 1938. The issue contained the first appearance of Superman, a character created by Jerry Siegel and Joe Shuster.

Many people use the term "graphic novel" to describe a series of short comics collected into a longer book. In 1978, Will Eisner's *A Contract with God* was the first book to label itself a graphic novel.

Today, many artists publish comics and graphic novels on the Internet. In 2004, Jeff Kinney started an original web book called *Diary of a Wimpy Kid*. In 2007, the book was published and became a *New York Times* best seller.

Discussion Questions

1. Instead of getting back at the bullies, Zack Allen chose to stop the runaway train. Why do you think he decided to use the Zinc Alloy suit for good instead of evil? Would you have made the same decision? Explain.

2. Each page of a graphic novel has several illustrations called panels. What is your favorite panel in this book? Describe what you like about the illustration and why it's your favorite.

3. *Robo Hero* is Zack Allen's favorite comic book. What is your favorite comic book or superhero? Describe why you like that book or character the best.

Writing Prompts

1. Imagine Zack Allen loaned you his Zinc Alloy suit for 24 hours. Write a story about your adventures. What would you do in the suit? Where would you go?

2. At the end of the story, the author hints that Zack will use the Zinc Alloy suit again. Write your own Zinc Alloy book. Who will he have to save next?

3. Many comic books are written and illustrated by two different people. Write a story, and then give it to a friend to illustrate.

Internet Sites

The book may be over, but the adventure is just beginning.

Do you want to read more about the subjects or ideas in this book? Want to play cool games or watch videos about the authors who write these books? Then go to FactHound. At *www.facthound.com*, you'll be able to do all that, and more. The FactHound website can also send you to other safe Internet sites.

Check it out!